Tales from Shakespeare

The Tempest
&
The Winter's Tale

悅讀莎士比亞故事 (7)

暴。風。雨。 &
冬。天。的。故。事。

Charles and Mary Lamb

CONTENTS

莎士比亞簡介 ……… 5

作者簡介：蘭姆姐弟 ……… 12

《暴風雨》導讀 ……… 16

《暴風雨》人物表 ……… 25

《暴風雨》故事內文 ……… 26

原劇本精彩擷句 ……… 74

CONTENTS

《冬天的故事》導讀……… 78

《冬天的故事》人物表……… 86

《冬天的故事》故事內文……… 88

原劇本精彩擷句 ……… 138

附本

《暴風雨》Practice

《冬天的故事》Practice

《暴風雨》中譯

《冬天的故事》中譯

威廉・莎士比亞（William Shakespeare, 1564-1616）

Shakespeare Centre, Henley St, Stratford-upon-Avon, Warwickshire

莎士比亞簡介

陳敬旻

威廉·莎士比亞（William Shakespeare）出生於英國的史特拉福（Stratford-upon-Avon）。莎士比亞的父親曾任地方議員，母親是地主的女兒。莎士比亞對婦女在廚房或起居室裡勞動的描繪不少，這大概是經由觀察母親所得。他本人也懂得園藝，故作品中的植草種樹表現鮮活。

1571 年，莎士比亞進入公立學校就讀，校內教學多採拉丁文，因此在其作品中到處可見到羅馬詩人奧維德（Ovid）的影子。當時代古典文學的英譯日漸普遍，有學者認為莎士比亞只懂得英語，但這種說法有可議之處。舉例來說，在高登的譯本裡，森林女神只用 Diana 這個名字，而莎士比亞卻在《仲夏夜之夢》一劇中用奧維德原作中的 Titania 一名來稱呼仙后。和莎士比亞有私交的文學家班·強生（Ben Jonson）則曾說，莎翁「懂得一點拉丁文，和一點點希臘文」。

莎士比亞的劇本亦常引用聖經典故，顯示他對新舊約也頗為熟悉。在伊麗莎白女王時期，通俗英語中已有很多聖經詞語。此外，莎士比亞應該很知悉當時代年輕人所流行的遊戲娛樂，當時也應該有巡迴劇團不時前來史特拉福演出。 1575 年，伊麗莎白女王來到郡上時，當地人以化裝遊行、假面戲劇、煙火來款待女王，《仲夏夜之夢》裡就有這種盛會的描繪。

1582 年，莎士比亞與安‧海瑟威（Anne Hathaway）結婚，但這場婚姻顯得草率，連莎士比亞的雙親都因不知情而沒有出席婚禮。1586 年，他們在倫敦定居下來。 1586 年的倫敦已是英國首都，年輕人莫不想在此大展抱負。史特拉福與倫敦之間的交通頻仍，但對身無長物的人而言，步行仍是最平常的旅行方式。伊麗莎白時期的文學家喜好步行， 1618 年，班‧強生就曾在倫敦與愛丁堡之間徒步來回。

莎士比亞初抵倫敦的史料不充足，引發諸多揣測。其中一說為莎士比亞曾在律師處當職員，因為他在劇本與詩歌中經常提及法律術語。但這種說法站不住腳，因為莎士比亞多有訛用，例如他在《威尼斯商人》和《一報還一報》中提到的法律原理及程序，就有諸多錯誤。

事實上，伊麗莎白時期的作家都喜歡引用法律詞彙，這是因為當時的文人和律師時有往來，而且中產階級也常介入訴訟案件，許多法律術語自然為常人所知。莎士比亞樂於援用法律術語，這顯示了他對當代生活和風尚的興趣。莎士比亞自抵達倫敦到告老還鄉，心思始終放在戲劇和詩歌上，不太可能接受法律這門專業領域的訓練。

莎士比亞在倫敦的第一份工作是劇場工作。當時常態營業的劇場有兩個：「劇場」（the Theatre）和「帷幕」（the Curtain）。「劇場」的所有人為詹姆士・波比奇（James Burbage），莎士比亞就在此落腳。「劇場」財務狀況不佳，1596 年波比奇過世，把「劇場」交給兩個兒子，其中一個兒子便是著名的悲劇演員理查・波比奇（Richard Burbage）。後來「劇場」因租約問題無法解決，決定將原有的建築物拆除，在泰晤士河的對面重建，改名為「環球」（the Globe）。不久，「環球」就展開了戲劇史上空前繁榮的時代。

伊麗莎白時期的戲劇表演只有男演員，所有的女性角色都由男性擔任。演員反串時會戴上面具，效果十足，然而這並不損故事的意境。莎士比亞本身也是一位出色的演員，曾在《皆大歡喜》和《哈姆雷特》中分別扮演忠僕亞當和國王鬼魂這兩個角色。

莎士比亞很留意演員的説白道詞，這點可從哈姆雷特告誡伶人的對話中窺知一二。莎士比亞熟稔劇場的技術與運作，加上他也是劇場股東，故對劇場的營運和組織都甚有研究。不過，他的志業不在演出或劇場管理，而是劇本和詩歌創作。

莎士比亞的戲劇創作始於 1591 年，他當時真正師法的對象是擅長喜劇的約翰・李利（John Lyly），以及曾寫下轟動一時的悲劇《帖木兒大帝》（*Tamburlaine the Great*）的克里斯多夫・馬婁（Christopher Marlowe）。莎翁戲劇的特色是兼容並蓄，吸收各家長處，而且他也勤奮多產。一直到 1611 年封筆之前，他每年平均寫出兩部劇作和三卷詩作。莎士比亞慣於在既有的文學作品中尋找材料，又重視大眾喜好，常能讓平淡無奇的作品廣受喜愛。

在當時代，劇本都是賣斷給劇場，不能再賣給出版商，因此莎劇的出版先後，並不能反映其創作的時間先後。莎翁作品的先後順序都由後人所推斷，推測的主要依據是作品題材和韻格。他早期的戲劇作品，無論悲劇或喜劇，性質都很單純。隨著創作的手法逐漸成熟，內容愈來愈複雜深刻，悲喜劇熔冶一爐。

自 1591 年席德尼爵士（Sir Philip Sidney）的十四行詩集發表後，十四行詩（sonnets，另譯為商籟）在英國即普遍受到文人的喜愛與仿傚。其中許多作品承續佩脫拉克（Petrarch）的風格，多描寫愛情的酸甜苦樂。莎士比亞的創作一向很能反應當時代的文學風尚，在詩歌體裁鼎盛之時，他也將才華展現在十四行詩上，並將部分作品寫入劇本之中。

莎士比亞的十四行詩主要有兩個主題：婚姻責任和詩歌的不朽。這兩者皆是文藝復興時期詩歌中常見的主題。不少人以為莎士比亞的十四行詩表達了他個人的自省與懺悔，但事實上這些內容有更多是源於他的戲劇天分。

1595 年至 1598 年，莎士比亞陸續寫了《羅密歐與茱麗葉》、《仲夏夜之夢》、《馴悍記》、《威尼斯商人》和若干歷史劇，他的詩歌戲劇也在這段時期受到肯定。當時代的梅爾斯（Francis Meres）就將莎士比亞視為最偉大的文學家，他說：「要是繆思會說英語，一定也會喜歡引用莎士比亞的精彩語藻。」「無論是悲劇或喜劇，莎士比亞的表現都是首屈一指。」

闊別故鄉十一年後，莎士比亞於 1596 年返回故居，並在隔年買下名為「新居」（New Place）的房子。那是鎮上第二大的房子，他大幅改建整修，爾後家道日益興盛。莎士比亞有足夠的財力置產並不足以為奇，但他大筆的固定收入主要來自表演，而非劇本創作。當時不乏有成功的演員靠演戲發財，甚至有人將這種現象寫成劇本。

除了表演之外，劇場行政及管理的工作，還有宮廷演出的賞賜，都是他的財源。許多文獻均顯示，莎士比亞是個非常關心財富、地產和社會地位的人，讓許多人感到與他的詩人形象有些扞格不入。

伊麗莎白女王過世後，詹姆士一世（James I）於 1603 年登基，他把莎士比亞所屬的劇團納入保護。莎士比亞此時寫了《第十二夜》和佳評如潮的《哈姆雷特》，成就傲視全英格蘭。但他仍謙恭有禮、溫文爾雅，一如十多年前初抵倫敦的樣子，因此也愈發受到大眾的喜愛。

從這一年起，莎士比亞開始撰寫悲劇《奧賽羅》。他寫悲劇並非是因為精神壓力或生活變故，而是身為一名劇作家，最終目的就是要寫出優秀的悲劇作品。當時他嘗試以詩入劇，在《哈姆雷特》和《一報還一報》中尤其爐火純青。隨後《李爾王》和《馬克白》問世，一直到四年後的《安東尼與克麗奧佩脫拉》，寫作風格登峰造極。

1609 年，倫敦瘟疫猖獗，隔年不見好轉，46 歲的莎士比亞決定告別倫敦，返回史特拉福退隱。 1616 年，莎士比亞和老友德雷頓、班·強生聚會時，可能由於喝得過於盡興，回家後發高熱，一病不起。他將遺囑修改完畢，同年 4 月 23 日，恰巧在他 52 歲的生日當天去世。

七年後，昔日的劇團好友收錄他的劇本做為全集出版，其中有喜劇、歷史劇、悲劇等共 36 個劇本。此書不僅不負莎翁本人所託，也為後人留下珍貴而豐富的文化資源，其中不僅包括美妙動人的詞句，還有各種人物的性格塑造，如高貴、低微、嚴肅或歡樂等性格的著墨。

除了作品，莎士比亞本人也在生前受到讚揚。班・強生曾說他是個「正人君子，天性開放自由，想像力出奇，擁有大無畏的思想，言詞溫和，蘊含機智。」也有學者以勇敢、敏感、平衡、幽默和身心健康這五種特質來形容莎士比亞，並說他「將無私的愛奉為至上，認為罪惡的根源是恐懼，而非金錢。」

值得一提的是，有人認為這些劇本刻畫入微，具有知性，不可能是未受過大學教育的莎士比亞所寫，因而引發爭議。有人就此推測真正的作者，其中較為人知的有法蘭西斯・培根（Francis Bacon）和牛津的德維爾公爵（Edward de Vere of Oxford），後者形成了頗具影響力的牛津學派。儘管傳說繪聲繪影，各種假說和研究不斷，但大概已經沒有人會懷疑確有莎士比亞這個人的存在了。

作者簡介：蘭姆姐弟

姐姐瑪麗（Mary Lamb）生於 1764 年，弟弟查爾斯（Charles Lamb）於 1775 年也在倫敦呱呱落地。因為家境不夠寬裕，瑪麗沒有接受過完整的教育。她從小就做針線活，幫忙持家，照顧母親。查爾斯在學生時代結識了詩人柯立芝（Samuel Taylor Coleridge），兩人成為終生的朋友。查爾斯後來因家中經濟困難而輟學， 1792 年轉而就職於東印度公司（East India House），這是他謀生的終身職業。

查爾斯在二十歲時一度精神崩潰，瑪麗則因為長年工作過量，在 1796 年突然精神病發，持刀攻擊父母，母親不幸傷重身亡。這件人倫悲劇發生後，瑪麗被判為精神異常，送往精神病院。查爾斯為此放棄自己原本期待的婚姻，以便全心照顧姐姐，使她免於在精神病院終老。

十九世紀的英國教育重視莎翁作品，一般的中產階級家庭也希望孩子早點接觸莎劇。1806 年，文學家兼編輯高德溫（William Godwin）邀請查爾斯協助「少年圖書館」的出版計畫，請他將莎翁的劇本改寫為適合兒童閱讀的故事。

查爾斯接受這項工作後就與瑪麗合作，他負責六齣悲劇，瑪麗負責十四齣喜劇並撰寫前言。瑪麗在後來曾描述說，他們兩人「就坐在同一張桌子上改寫，看起來就好像《仲夏夜之夢》裡的荷米雅與海蓮娜一樣。」就這樣，姐弟兩人合力完成了這一系列的莎士比亞故事。《莎士比亞故事集》在 1807 年出版後便大受好評，建立了查爾斯的文學聲譽。

查爾斯的寫作風格獨特，筆法樸實，主題豐富。他將自己的一生，包括童年時代、基督教會學校的生活、東印度公司的光陰、與瑪麗相伴的點點滴滴，以及自己的白日夢、鍾愛的書籍和友人等等，都融入在文章裡，作品充滿細膩情感和豐富的想像力。他的軟弱、怪異、魅力、幽默、口吃，在在都使讀者感到親切熟悉，而獨特的筆法與敘事方式，也使他成為英國出色的散文大師。

1823 年，查爾斯和瑪麗領養了一個孤兒愛瑪。兩年後，查爾斯自東印度公司退休，獲得豐厚的退休金。查爾斯的健康情形和瑪麗的精神狀況卻每況愈下。 1833 年，愛瑪嫁給出版商後，又只剩下姐弟兩人。 1834 年 7 月，由於幼年時代的好友柯立芝去世，查爾斯的精神一蹶不振，沉湎酒精。此年秋天，查爾斯在散步時不慎跌倒，傷及顏面，後來傷口竟惡化至不可收拾的地步，而於年底過世。

查爾斯善與人交，他和同時期的許多文人都保持良好情誼，又因他一生對姐姐的照顧不餘遺力，所以也廣受敬佩。查爾斯和瑪麗兩人都終生未婚，查爾斯曾在一篇伊利亞小品中，將他們的狀況形容為「雙重單身」（double singleness）。查爾斯去世後，瑪麗的心理狀態雖然漸趨惡化，但仍繼續活了十三年之久。

The Tempest

暴風雨

導讀

陳敬旻

《暴風雨》（*The Tempest*）是《莎士比亞全集》初版第一對開本裡的第一齣喜劇。此劇完成於 1611 年，同年 11 月在白廳（White Hall）於詹姆士國王御前演出。 1613 年，莎士比亞的劇團再度受命演出此劇，以慶祝國王的女兒伊麗莎白出閣。這個劇本載歌載舞，戲劇效果佳，極適合在婚宴上演出。

魔法的劇情

本故事內容發生在一座杳無人煙的小島，主要角色普洛斯（Prospero）精通魔法，整齣戲就是由他透過法力「自編自導」而成，其中有引人入勝的狂風暴雨、千奇百變的魔幻法術、飛舞的隱形精靈、怪異畸形的半人半獸，還有奇妙有趣的純情故事等。

《暴風雨》和《連環錯》（*The Comedy of Errors*）一樣，都是莎劇中罕見吻合三一律的劇本——故事的地點都發生在荒島上，所有的事情都發生在同一天，並獲得圓滿結局。

《暴風雨》一劇追溯到幕啟前十二年，原為米蘭公爵的普洛斯因鑽研法術，埋首書堆，荒於政務，把王國轉交給弟弟安東尼（Antonio）代管。沒想到安東尼執政一段時日後，就與那不勒斯王聯合起來篡奪爵位，然後棄普洛斯和與其年幼的女兒米蘭達（Miranda）於大海上。

隨後父女兩人漂流至荒島，後來普洛斯盼到最佳時機，當年出賣他的弟弟和那不勒斯王，如今帶領一群隨行人員往荒島駛來。於是他掀起一場暴風雨，以便讓兩人後悔當年所犯的過錯，最後並完成了米蘭達的婚事。

奇幻島的主題

奇幻島在民間文學中並不是罕見的主題，但當時的新聞時事可能才是莎士比亞最重要的靈感來源。 1609 年初夏，英國維吉尼亞公司（Virginia Company）的一艘巨大艦隊滿載四百多人，準備由普利茅斯（Plymouth）啟航，前往殖民地維吉尼亞州的詹姆士鎮（Jamestown）。未料七月某日發生強烈颶風，沖散艦隊，所幸所有艦隊船艇都在八月安全抵達詹姆士鎮，除了失去音訊的「海洋冒險號」（Sea Adventure）。

大家都認為「海洋冒險號」船上的人員凶多吉少，恐怕全數罹難。然而，就在隔年的五月，竟有兩艘小艇載著全數存活的「海洋冒險號」人員，奇蹟似地抵達詹姆士鎮，令眾人驚嘆不已。原來，他們一行人遇到船難後，無意間登陸維吉尼亞海岸旁的百慕達島（Bermuda），因而保住了性命。

這座島嶼是當時水手口中聲名狼藉的惡魔島（Isle of Devils），船隻莫不避之，直到「海洋冒險號」抵達後，才發現那裡是人間仙境。那裡不但食宿無慮，島上也有豐富的木材供搭建船艇。這則消息一經披露，便引起轟動，「海洋冒險號」上的人也紛紛寫下這段奇異旅程。其中莎翁所閱讀到的，可能是由船上秘書史崔奇（William Strachey）在 1610 年 7 月 15 日所寫的船難獲救紀實手稿。

《暴風雨》中的島嶼約位於今日的地中海，介於突尼斯（Tunis）和那不勒斯（Naples）之間，除了「海洋冒險號」登陸百慕達的事件，劇中的這座荒島也有美洲新大陸的色彩。法國人文思想家蒙田（Montaigne）寫過一篇文章，名為〈Of the Cannibals〉（但 cannibal 一字當時並沒有「食人肉」之意），內容在於歌頌美洲印第安族群的生活。

蒙田（Michel de Montaigne, 1533-1592）認為他們與大自然融合，簡單純樸，沒有政治紛擾和貧富問題，生活悠閒、平等、自然，彷彿就像柏拉圖的理想國，是一種完美理想的境界。〈Of the Cannibals〉的英文版在 1603 年出版，莎士比亞應該也看過這篇文章，因為第一對開本中的人物表，莎士比亞將卡力班描述成一個「野蠻畸形的奴隸」，而卡力班的名字 Caliban 就是由 Cannibal 裡的兩個子音對調而來的。

「技藝」與「自然」

《暴風雨》最重要的一個主題，就是「技藝」（art）與「自然」（nature）的分別。

普洛斯所擁有的魔法是一種技藝，具有改變自然的力量。他的法力無邊，結合魔法與威權，主宰所有人的生命及意志：包括女兒米蘭達、活潑精靈艾瑞爾（Ariel）、半人半獸的怪物卡力班（Caliban），以及斐迪南（Ferdinand）和那不勒斯王一行人。「自然」在中古暨文藝復興時期的意思是「種類」（kind），故「人性」（human nature）暗指人性千種萬類。

CALIBAN:-AS I TOLD THEE BEFORE I AM SUBJECT TO A TYRANT: A SORCERER-(ACT III S)

人性有高貴的一面，例如忠心護主的剛則婁（Gonzalo），也有卑劣的一面，例如篡位、陷害兄長的安東尼，於此，「保有自然本性」和「合乎道德」兩種目標就可能衝突。普洛斯藉由外力，讓船上一干人飽受重重的心理試煉，如焦慮、誘惑、悲慟、恐懼、懺悔等，使他們改邪歸正，自己也重拾了爵位。

一場驚天動地的暴風雨，最後成為重生與覺悟的序曲，終而一片和諧，諸如此類的轉折與結局，都是典型的莎士比亞風格。

「奴役」與「自由」

　　普洛斯對艾瑞爾和卡力班的控制，觸及了「奴役」與「自由」的問題。

普洛斯最得力的助手就是艾瑞爾，但艾瑞爾是個精靈，不屬於人類，他來去自如、不受拘束。他之所以服侍普洛斯，是為了要報恩。艾瑞爾一角和《仲夏夜之夢》（*A Midsummer Night's Dream*）裡的精靈帕克相仿，但兩者的個性天差地別。

普洛斯恩威並重，以紀律和記憶控制住艾瑞爾。命運截然不同的卡力班，則是另一個受到奴役的代表，他是女巫辛蔻雷（Sycorax）的兒子，比艾瑞爾接近人類，普洛斯有意教化他，卻徒勞無功。

米蘭達是卡力班的相反典型，她天性善良溫馴，讓斐迪南一見到她就誤以為她是女神。在米蘭達的眼中，初見的人事物莫不美好，當她見到那不勒斯王和安東尼一群人時，說道：

> O brave new world, that has such people in it.
> 啊！美麗的新世界，裡頭有如此這般的人們！

十九世紀的赫胥黎（Aldous Leonard Huxley, 1894-1963）引用了「美麗新世界」（Brave New World）來做書名，這一個詞語從此也幾乎就人盡皆知了。

「馬格斯」魔法師

普洛斯掀起的暴風雨雖然威力驚人，但本意並不在傷人。儘管復仇者心懷深怨重恨，莎士比亞卻盡力不讓普洛斯表現出多年的舊仇，而且在普洛斯達成目的後，就讓他棄絕魔法，表現出自制力。莎士比亞時期的人稱偉大的魔法師為「馬格斯」（magus），大眾很著迷馬格斯這種人物。這種人物的特質是博學多聞、克勤律己、耐心求藝，因為惟有如此，才足以召喚自然界與超自然界的神秘力量。

馬格斯不像鄉野荒郊間的巫婆，以療傷治病為號召或做些小奸小惡之事，也不像汲汲營營於化物成金的煉金師。馬格斯的形象是身穿織有神秘象徵的長袍，他們具有哲思智慧，行善必有善報。

儘管如此，當時的人提到馬格斯時，心頭仍不免有所餘悸，因為當時名聲最好的馬格斯約翰・迪伊（John Dee, 1527-1608），他是伊麗莎白一世的顧問。他後來從自己家中的藏書室（也是英格蘭最大的私人圖書館）出走，焚身而亡。

John Dee, 1527-1608

22

浪漫劇

後世的批評家一向把《暴風雨》視為「浪漫劇」（romance），莎翁晚期的作品幾乎都是浪漫劇，年代更早的《冬天的故事》（*The Winter's Tale*）也是。《暴風雨》的故事情節呼應了若干浪漫劇中常見的主題，例如：

▪ 父親對女兒的控制或依戀	《奧賽羅》《李爾王》
▪ 叛君行為	《哈姆雷特》《馬克白》
▪ 由宮廷至荒野，再回返宮廷的過程	《仲夏夜之夢》
	《皆大歡喜》
▪ 藉由技術特別是戲中戲來操控他人	《無事生非》
	《哈姆雷特》
▪ 天性與教養的區別	《冬天的故事》
▪ 魔法的魅力	《仲夏夜之夢》

《暴風雨》是莎翁獨自創作的最後一齣劇本，十九世紀以降，就不乏將普洛斯視為莎翁化身的揣測。持此觀點的人認為莎翁就是以本劇告別劇場，而普洛斯在劇終將「魔法書和魔杖深埋地底下」，彷彿是莎翁離開劇場的心聲。雖然反對意見認為，莎翁鮮少將自己與劇中人物混為一談，更何況普洛斯是一個遭人放逐、懷恨在心、控制欲強的巫師。不過，劇場天地和魔法幻覺一樣，終究是以真實世界為基礎，故仍有人將普洛斯的魔法視為莎士比亞的生花妙筆。

二十世紀後，學術界開始以「殖民主義」（普洛斯與卡力班的主僕關係）和「女性主義」的觀點（普洛斯與米蘭達的父女關係）來探討《暴風雨》。一九九○年代，英國導演彼得·格林那威（Peter Greenaway）執導的電影《魔法師的寶典》（*Prospero's Books*），便是改編自《暴風雨》。電影由英國實力派演員約翰·吉爾格爵士（Sir John Gielgud）擔任普洛斯一角，當時他已年過八旬，戲劇生涯超過一甲子，而且還是個資歷豐富、演技精湛的莎劇演員，由他來飾演普洛斯，使觀眾不得不聯想到吉爾格、普洛斯、莎士比亞三人是否在劇場的魔法圈內，也有著微妙的交集。有興趣的讀者不妨參考之。

人物表

Prospero 普洛斯 米蘭公爵

Miranda 米蘭達 普洛斯之女

Ariel 艾瑞爾 精靈

Caliban 卡力班 普洛斯的僕人

Antonio 安東尼 普洛斯的弟弟，篡權者

Ferdinand 斐迪南 那不勒斯王子

Gonzalo 剛則婁 國王的臣子，曾幫助普
洛斯

Sycorax 辛蔻雷 女巫

The Tempest

There was a certain island in the sea, the only inhabitants of which were an old man, whose name was Prospero, and his daughter Miranda, a very beautiful young lady. She came to this island so young, that she had no memory of having seen any other human face than her father's.

They lived in a cave or cell, made out of a rock; it was divided into several apartments, one of which Prospero called his study; there he kept his books, which chiefly treated of magic, a study at that time much affected by all learned men: and the knowledge of this art he found very useful to him; for being thrown by a strange chance upon this island, which had been enchanted[1] by a witch called Sycorax, who died there a short time before his arrival, Prospero, by virtue of his art, released many good spirits that Sycorax had imprisoned in the bodies of large trees, because they had refused to execute her wicked commands. These gentle spirits were ever after obedient to the will of Prospero. Of these Ariel was the chief.

---

1 enchant [ɪnˈtʃænt] (v.) 施魔法

🎧2 The lively little sprite Ariel had nothing mischievous in his nature, except that he took rather too much pleasure in tormenting an ugly monster called Caliban, for he owed him a grudge[2] because he was the son of his old enemy Sycorax.

2 grudge [grʌdʒ] (n.) 怨恨；嫌隙

THE BANISHED DUKE.

This Caliban, Prospero found in the woods, a strange misshapen thing, far less human in form than an ape: he took him home to his cell, and taught him to speak; and Prospero would have been very kind to him, but the bad nature which Caliban inherited[3] from his mother, Sycorax, would not let him learn anything good or useful: therefore he was employed like a slave, to fetch wood and do the most laborious offices; and Ariel had the charge of compelling[4] him to these services.

3 inherit [ɪnˈherɪt] (v.) 繼承；得自遺傳
4 compel [kəmˈpel] (v.) 強迫

When Caliban was lazy and neglected his work, Ariel (who was invisible to all eyes but Prospero's) would come slily and pinch[5] him, and sometimes tumble[6] him down in the mire[7]; and then Ariel, in the likeness of an ape, would make mouths at him. Then swiftly changing his shape, in the likeness of a hedgehog[8], he would lie tumbling in Caliban's way, who feared the hedgehog's sharp quills[9] would prick his bare feet. With a variety of suchlike vexatious[10] tricks Ariel would often torment him, whenever Caliban neglected the work which Prospero commanded him to do.

Having these powerful spirits obedient to his will, Prospero could by their means command the winds, and the waves of the sea. By his orders they raised a violent storm, in the midst of which, and struggling with the wild sea-waves that every moment threatened to swallow it up, he showed his daughter a fine large ship, which he told her was full of living beings like themselves.

5 pinch [pɪntʃ] (v.) 捏；擰
6 tumble [ˈtʌmbəl] (v.) 使跌倒
7 mire [maɪr] (n.) 泥坑
8 hedgehog [ˈhedʒhɑːg] (n.) 刺蝟
9 quill [kwɪl] (n.) 豪豬堅硬的長刺
10 vexatious [vekˈseɪʃəs] (a.) 令人煩惱的

🎧 5 "O my dear father," said she, "if by your art you have raised this dreadful storm, have pity on their sad distress. See! the vessel[11] will be dashed[12] to pieces. Poor souls! they will all perish[13]. If I had power, I would sink the sea beneath the earth, rather than the good ship should be destroyed, with all the precious souls within her."

11 vessel ['vesəl] (n.) 船；船艦
12 dash [dæʃ] (v.) 猛撞；撞擊
13 perish ['perɪʃ] (v.) 毀滅；死亡

Miranda.   Oh, woe the day!
Prospero.   No harm.
I have done nothing but in care of thee,—
Of thee, my dear one! thee, my daughter.

Act I.   Scene II.

"Be not so amazed, daughter Miranda," said Prospero; "there is no harm done. I have so ordered it, that no person in the ship shall receive any hurt. What I have done has been in care of you, my dear child. You are ignorant who you are, or where you came from, and you know no more of me, but that I am your father, and live in this poor cave. Can you remember a time before you came to this cell? I think you cannot, for you were not then three years of age."

"Certainly I can, sir," replied Miranda.

"By what?" asked Prospero; "by any other house or person? Tell me what you can remember, my child."

Miranda said: "It seems to me like the recollection[14] of a dream. But had I not once four or five women who attended upon me?"

Prospero answered: "You had, and more. How is it that this still lives in your mind? Do you remember how you came here?"

"No, sir," said Miranda, "I remember nothing more."

14 recollection [ˌrekəˈlekʃən] (n.) 記憶

🎧7 "Twelve years ago, Miranda," continued Prospero, "I was Duke of Milan, and you were a princess, and my only heir[15]. I had a younger brother, whose name was Antonio, to whom I trusted everything; and as I was fond of retirement and deep study, I commonly left the management of my state affairs to your uncle, my false brother (for so indeed he proved). I, neglecting all worldly ends, buried among my books, did dedicate my whole time to the bettering of my mind. My brother Antonio being thus in possession of my power, began to think himself the duke indeed. The opportunity I gave him of making himself popular among my subjects awakened in his bad nature a proud ambition to deprive[16] me of my dukedom: this he soon effected with the aid of the King of Naples, a powerful prince, who was my enemy."

"Wherefore," said Miranda, "did they not that hour destroy us?"

15 heir [er] (n.) 繼承人
16 deprive [dɪ'praɪv] (v.) 剝奪；使喪失

🎧8 "My child," answered her father, "they durst[17] not, so dear was the love that my people bore me. Antonio carried us on board a ship, and when we were some leagues[18] out at sea, he forced us into a small boat, without either tackle[19], sail, or mast[20]: there he left us, as he thought, to perish. But a kind lord of my court, one Gonzalo, who loved me, had privately placed in the boat, water, provisions[21], apparel, and some books which I prize above my dukedom."

"O my father," said Miranda, "what a trouble must I have been to you then!"

17 durst [dɜːrst] (v.)〔古〕dare 的過去式
18 league [liːg] (n.)〔舊〕海哩
19 tackle ['tækəl] (n.)（用來操縱船帆或吊起重物等的）滑車
20 mast [mæst] (n.) 船桅
21 provisions [prə'vɪʒənz] (n.)〔作複數形〕食物；食物供應

PROS:⟨ BY ACCIDENT MOST STRANGE, BOUNTIFUL FORTUNE,
PERO⟨ NOW MY DEAR LADY, HATH MINE ENEMIES
BROUGHT TO THIS SHORE;— »

"No, my love," said Prospero, "you were a little cherub[22] that did preserve me. Your innocent smiles made me bear up against my misfortunes. Our food lasted till we landed on this desert island, since when my chief delight has been in teaching you, Miranda, and well have you profited by my instructions."

"Heaven thank you, my dear father," said Miranda. "Now pray tell me, sir, your reason for raising this sea-storm?"

"Know then," said her father, "that by means of this storm, my enemies, the King of Naples, and my cruel brother, are cast ashore upon this island."

22 cherub ['tʃerəb] (n.) 天真無邪的可愛孩童

Having so said, Prospero gently touched his daughter with his magic wand, and she fell fast asleep; for the spirit Ariel just then presented himself before his master, to give an account of the tempest, and how he had disposed[23] of the ship's company, and though the spirits were always invisible to Miranda, Prospero did not choose she should hear him holding converse (as would seem to her) with the empty air.

"Well, my brave spirit," said Prospero to Ariel, "how have you performed your task?"

Ariel gave a lively description of the storm, and of the terrors of the mariners, and how the king's son, Ferdinand, was the first who leaped into the sea; and his father thought he saw his dear son swallowed up by the waves and lost.

23 dispose [dɪˈspoʊz] (v.) 處理；處置

BOATSWAIN: "HENCE! WHAT CARE THESE ROARERS FOR THE NAME OF KING?"

🎧 11 "But he is safe," said Ariel, "in a corner of the isle, sitting with his arms folded, sadly lamenting[24] the loss of the king, his father, whom he concludes drowned. Not a hair of his head is injured, and his princely garments, though drenched in the sea-waves, look fresher than before."

"That's my delicate Ariel," said Prospero. "Bring him hither: my daughter must see this young prince. Where is the king, and my brother?"

"I left them," answered Ariel, "searching for Ferdinand, whom they have little hopes of finding, thinking they saw him perish. Of the ship's crew not one is missing; though each one thinks himself the only one saved; and the ship, though invisible to them, is safe in the harbor."

"Ariel," said Prospero, "thy charge is faithfully performed: but there is more work yet."

"Is there more work?" said Ariel. "Let me remind you, master, you have promised me my liberty. I pray, remember, I have done you worthy service, told you no lies, made no mistakes, served you without grudge or grumbling[25]."

24 lament [ləˈment] (v.) 悲傷；惋惜
25 grumble [ˈgrʌmbəl] (v.) 抱怨；牢騷

THE WANDERERS.

🎧 ⒓ "How now!" said Prospero. "You do not recollect what a torment I freed you from. Have you forgot the wicked witch Sycorax, who with age and envy was almost bent double? Where was she born? Speak; tell me."

"Sir, in Algiers," said Ariel.

"O was she so?" said Prospero. "I must recount[26] what you have been, which I find you do not remember. This bad witch, Sycorax, for her witchcrafts, too terrible to enter human hearing, was banished[27] from Algiers, and here left by the sailors; and because you were a spirit too delicate to execute her wicked commands, she shut you up in a tree, where I found you howling[28]. This torment, remember, I did free you from."

"Pardon me, dear master," said Ariel, ashamed to seem ungrateful; "I will obey your commands."

"Do so," said Prospero, "and I will set you free." He then gave orders what further he would have him do; and away went Ariel, first to where he had left Ferdinand, and found him still sitting on the grass in the same melancholy posture.

26 recount [rɪˈkaʊnt] (v.) 講述
27 banish [ˈbænɪʃ] (v.) 放逐;驅逐出境
28 howl [haʊl] (v.) 哀嚎

44

"O my young gentleman," said Ariel, when he saw him, "I will soon move you. You must be brought, I find, for the Lady Miranda to have a sight of your pretty person. Come. sir, follow me." He then began singing:

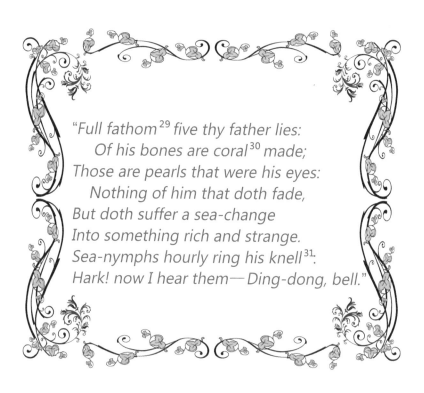

"Full fathom[29] five thy father lies:
Of his bones are coral[30] made;
Those are pearls that were his eyes:
Nothing of him that doth fade,
But doth suffer a sea-change
Into something rich and strange.
Sea-nymphs hourly ring his knell[31].
Hark! now I hear them—Ding-dong, bell."

29 fathom [ˈfæðəm] (n.) 噚（測水深的單位，一噚是 1.829 公尺）
30 coral [ˈkɑːrəl] (n.) 珊瑚
31 knell [nel] (n.) 鐘聲；喪鐘聲

Ariel's Song to Ferdinand

Ariell Song. Full fadom fiue thy Father lies,
Of his bones are Corrall made:
Those are pearles that were his eies,
Nothing of him that doth fade,
But doth suffer a Sea-change
Into something rich, & strange:
Sea-Nimphs hourly ring his knell.

This strange news of his lost father soon roused the prince from the stupid fit into which he had fallen. He followed in amazement the sound of Ariel's voice, till it led him to Prospero and Miranda, who were sitting under the shade of a large tree. Now Miranda had never seen a man before, except her own father.

"Miranda," said Prospero, "tell me what you are looking at yonder[32]."

"O father," said Miranda, in a strange surprise, "surely that is a spirit. Lord! how it looks about! Believe me, sir, it is a beautiful creature. Is it not a spirit?"

"No, girl," answered her father; "it eats, and sleeps, and has senses such as we have. This young man you see was in the ship. He is somewhat altered by grief, or you might call him a handsome person. He has lost his companions, and is wandering about to find them."

---

32 yonder ['jɑːndər] (adv.) 〔文〕那邊的；遠處（而可見）的

15 Miranda, who thought all men had grave faces and grey beards like her father, was delighted with the appearance of this beautiful young prince; and Ferdinand, seeing such a lovely lady in this desert place, and from the strange sounds he had heard, expecting nothing but wonders, thought he was upon an enchanted island, and that Miranda was the goddess of the place, and as such he began to address her.

She timidly answered, she was no goddess, but a simple maid, and was going to give him an account of herself, when Prospero interrupted her. He was well pleased to find they admired each other, for he plainly perceived they had (as we say) fallen in love at first sight: but to try Ferdinand's constancy[33], he resolved to throw some difficulties in their way: therefore, advancing forward, he addressed the prince with a stern[34] air, telling him, he came to the island as a spy, to take it from him who was the lord of it.

33 constancy [ˈkɑːnstənsi] (n.) 堅定不移；恆久不變
34 stern [stɜːrn] (a.) 嚴格的；嚴厲的

FERDINAND:— MOST SURE, THE GODDESS
ON WHOM THESE AIRS ATTEND!— (ACT I. SC. II)

"Follow me," said he. "I will tie your neck and feet together. You shall drink sea-water; shellfish, withered roots, and husks[35] of acorns shall be your food."

"No," said Ferdinand, "I will resist such entertainment, till I see a more powerful enemy," and drew his sword; but Prospero, waving his magic wand, fixed him to the spot where he stood, so that he had no power to move.

Miranda hung upon her father, saying: "Why are you so ungentle? Have pity, sir; I will be his surety[36]. This is the second man I ever saw, and to me he seems a true one."

35 husk [hʌsk] (n.) 外殼
36 surety ['sʊrɪti] (n.) 保證人

🎧17 "Silence," said the father: "one word more will make me chide[37] you, girl! What! an advocate for an impostor[38]! You think there are no more such fine men, having seen only him and Caliban. I tell you, foolish girl, most men as far excel this, as he does Caliban." This he said to prove his daughter's constancy; and she replied,

"My affections are most humble. I have no wish to see a goodlier man."

"Come on, young man," said Prospero to the Prince; "you have no power to disobey me."

37 chide [tʃaɪd] (v.) 〔文〕責罵;斥責
38 impostor [ɪmˈpɑːstər] (n.) 冒充者;騙子

"I have not indeed," answered Ferdinand; and not knowing that it was by magic he was deprived of all power of resistance, he was astonished to find himself so strangely compelled to follow Prospero: looking back on Miranda as long as he could see her, he said, as he went after Prospero into the cave, "My spirits are all bound up, as if I were in a dream; but this man's threats, and the weakness which I feel, would seem light to me if from my prison I might once a day behold this fair maid."

Prospero kept Ferdinand not long confined[39] within the cell: he soon brought out his prisoner, and set him a severe task to perform, taking care to let his daughter know the hard labour he had imposed[40] on him, and then pretending to go into his study, he secretly watched them both.

---

39 confine [kənˈfaɪn] (v.) 關起來
40 impose [ɪmˈpoʊz] (v.) 加（負擔等）於；強加於

MIRANDA: "IF YOU'LL SIT DOWN,
I'LL BEAR YOUR LOGS THE WHILE. PRAY GIVE ME THAT.
I'LL CARRY IT TO THE PILE."
ACT·III·SC·I·

Prospero had commanded Ferdinand to pile up some heavy logs of wood. Kings' sons not being much used to laborious work, Miranda soon after found her lover almost dying with fatigue.

"Alas!" said she, "do not work so hard; my father is at his studies, he is safe for these three hours; pray rest yourself."

"O my dear lady," said Ferdinand, "I dare not. I must finish my task before I take my rest."

"If you will sit down," said Miranda, "I will carry your logs the while."

But this Ferdinand would by no means agree to. Instead of a help Miranda became a hindrance[41], for they began a long conversation, so that the business of log-carrying went on very slowly.

Prospero, who had enjoined Ferdinand this task merely as a trial of his love, was not at his books, as his daughter supposed, but was standing by them invisible, to overhear what they said.

Ferdinand inquired her name, which she told, saying it was against her father's express command she did so.

41 hindrance ['hɪndrəns] (n.) 妨礙的人或物

THE PRINCE IN SERVITUDE.

[20] Prospero only smiled at this first instance of his daughter's disobedience, for having by his magic art caused his daughter to fall in love so suddenly, he was not angry that she showed her love by forgetting to obey his commands. And he listened well pleased to a long speech of Ferdinand's, in which he professed to love her above all the ladies he ever saw.

🎧 21 In answer to his praises of her beauty, which he said exceeded all the women in the world, she replied, "I do not remember the face of any woman, nor have I seen any more men than you, my good friend, and my dear father. How features are abroad, I know not; but, believe me, sir, I would not wish any companion in the world but you, nor can my imagination form any shape but yours that I could like. But, sir, I fear I talk to you too freely, and my father's precepts[42] I forget."

At this Prospero smiled, and nodded his head, as much as to say, "This goes on exactly as I could wish; my girl will be Queen of Naples."

---

42 precept [ˈpriːsept] (n.)（尤指行為的）規範；教訓

And then Ferdinand, in another fine long speech (for young princes speak in courtly phrases), told the innocent Miranda he was heir to the crown of Naples, and that she should be his queen.

"Ah! sir," said she, "I am a fool to weep at what I am glad of. I will answer you in plain and holy innocence. I am your wife if you will marry me."

Prospero prevented Ferdinand's thanks by appearing visible before them.

"Fear nothing, my child," said he; "I have overheard, and approve of all you have said. And, Ferdinand, if I have too severely used you, I will make you rich amends[43], by giving you my daughter. All your vexations were but trials of your love, and you have nobly stood the test. Then as my gift, which your true love has worthily purchased, take my daughter, and do not smile that I boast she is above all praise."

---

43 amends [əˈmendz] (n.)（作複數形）賠罪；賠償

He then, telling them that he had business which required his presence, desired they would sit down and talk together till he returned; and this command Miranda seemed not at all disposed to disobey.

When Prospero left them, he called his spirit Ariel, who quickly appeared before him, eager to relate what he had done with Prospero's brother and the King of Naples.

Ariel said he had left them almost out of their senses with fear, at the strange things he had caused them to see and hear. When fatigued with wandering about, and famished[44] for want of food, he had suddenly set before them a delicious banquet, and then, just as they were going to eat, he appeared visible before them in the shape of a harpy[45], a voracious[46] monster with wings, and the feast vanished away.

44 famish ['fæmɪʃ] (v.) 挨餓
45 harpy ['hɑːrpi] (n.) 〔希臘神話〕有女性面孔、長有鳥翅和爪子的 殘暴怪物
46 voracious [vɔː'reɪʃəs] (a.) 狼吞虎嚥的；貪婪的

THE FAIRY BANQUET.

🎧 24 Then, to their utter amazement, this seeming harpy spoke to them, reminding them of their cruelty in driving Prospero from his dukedom, and leaving him and his infant daughter to perish in the sea; saying, that for this cause these terrors were suffered to afflict[47] them.

The King of Naples, and Antonio the false brother, repented the injustice they had done to Prospero, and Ariel told his master he was certain their penitence[48] was sincere, and that he, though a spirit, could not but pity them.

"Then bring them hither, Ariel," said Prospero: "if you, who are but a spirit, feel for their distress, shall not I, who am a human being like themselves, have compassion on them? Bring them, quickly, my dainty[49] Ariel."

Ariel soon returned with the king, Antonio, and old Gonzalo in their train, who had followed him, wondering at the wild music he played in the air to draw them on to his master's presence. This Gonzalo was the same who had so kindly provided Prospero formerly with books and provisions, when his wicked brother left him, as he thought, to perish in an open boat in the sea.

---

47 afflict [əˈflɪkt] (v.) 使痛苦；折磨
48 penitence [ˈpenɪtəns] (n.) 懺悔；贖罪
49 dainty [ˈdeɪnti] (a.) 美麗的；優雅的

🎧25 Grief and terror had so stupefied[50] their senses, that they did not know Prospero. He first discovered himself to the good old Gonzalo, calling him the preserver of his life; and then his brother and the king knew that he was the injured Prospero.

Antonio, with tears and sad words of sorrow and true repentance, implored[51] his brother's forgiveness, and the king expressed his sincere remorse[52] for having assisted Antonio to depose[53] his brother: and Prospero forgave them; and, upon their engaging to restore his dukedom, he said to the King of Naples, "I have a gift in store for you too;" and opening a door, showed him his son Ferdinand playing at chess with Miranda.

50 stupefy ['stuːpɪfaɪ] (v.) 使驚呆
51 implore [ɪmˈplɔːr] (v.) 懇求
52 remorse [rɪˈmɔːrs] (n.) 懊悔；自責
53 depose [dɪˈpoʊz] (v.) 迫使下台

THE LOST PRINCE.

🎧26   Nothing could exceed the joy of the father and the son at this unexpected meeting, for they each thought the other drowned in the storm.

"O wonder!" said Miranda, "what noble creatures there are! It must surely be a brave world that has such people in it."

MIRANDA. SWEET LORD YOU PLAY ME FALSE.
FERDINAND.   NO MY DEAREST LOVE
I WOULD NOT FOR THE WORLD.   ACT V. SC. 1.

The King of Naples was almost as much astonished at the beauty and excellent graces of the young Miranda, as his son had been. "Who is this maid?" said he; "she seems the goddess that has parted us, and brought us thus together."

"No, sir," answered Ferdinand, smiling to find his father had fallen into the same mistake that he had done when he first saw Miranda, "she is a mortal, but by immortal Providence[54] she is mine; I chose her when I could not ask you, my father, for your consent[55], not thinking you were alive. She is the daughter to this Prospero, who is the famous Duke of Milan, of whose renown I have heard so much, but never saw him till now: of him I have received a new life: he has made himself to me a second father, giving me this dear lady."

"Then I must be her father," said the king; "but oh! how oddly will it sound, that I must ask my child forgiveness."

"No more of that," said Prospero: "let us not remember our troubles past, since they so happily have ended."

---

54 Providence ['prɑːvɪdəns] (n.)（作大寫）上帝；老天爺
55 consent [kən'sent] (v.) 同意；答應

🎧28 And then Prospero embraced his brother, and again assured him of his forgiveness; and said that a wise overruling Providence had permitted that he should be driven from his poor dukedom of Milan, that his daughter might inherit the crown of Naples, for that by their meeting in this desert island, it had happened that the king's son had loved Miranda.

These kind words which Prospero spoke, meaning to comfort his brother, so filled Antonio with shame and remorse, that he wept and was unable to speak; and the kind old Gonzalo wept to see this joyful reconciliation[56], and prayed for blessings on the young couple.

Prospero now told them that their ship was safe in the harbour, and the sailors all on board her, and that he and his daughter would accompany them home the next morning.

"In the meantime," says he, "partake[57] of such refreshments as my poor cave affords; and for your evening's entertainment I will relate the history of my life from my first landing in this desert island."

---

56 reconciliation [ˌrekənsɪliˈeɪʃən] (n.) 和解
57 partake [pɑːrˈteɪk] (v.) 分享；分擔

He then called for Caliban to prepare some food, and set the cave in order; and the company were astonished at the uncouth[58] form and savage appearance of this ugly monster, who (Prospero said) was the only attendant he had to wait upon him.

Before Prospero left the island, he dismissed Ariel from his service, to the great joy of that lively little spirit; who, though he had been a faithful servant to his master, was always longing to enjoy his free liberty, to wander uncontrolled in the air, like a wild bird, under green trees, among pleasant fruits, and sweet-smelling flowers.

58 uncouth [ʌnˈkuːθ] (a.) 粗魯的；沒教養的

AMONG THE FLOWERS.

"My quaint[59] Ariel," said Prospero to the little sprite[60] when he made him free, "I shall miss you; yet you shall have your freedom."

"Thank you, my dear master;" said Ariel; "but give me leave to attend your ship home with prosperous gales[61], before you bid farewell to the assistance of your faithful spirit; and then, master, when I am free, how merrily I shall live!" Here Ariel sung this pretty song:

59 quaint [kweɪnt] (a.) 古怪的
60 sprite [spraɪt] (n.) 精靈
61 gale [geɪl] (n.) 大風;強風

🎧31 "Where the bee sucks, there suck I;
In a cowslip's[62] bell I lie:
There I crouch[63] when owls do cry.
On the bat's back I do fly
After summer Merrily.
Merrily, merrily shall I live now
Under the blossom that hangs on the bough."

62 cowslip ['kaʊˌslɪp] (n.) 野櫻草
63 crouch [kraʊtʃ] (v.) 蹲伏

THE·DANCE·OF·THE·NYMPHS·&·THE·REAPERS
ACT IV. SC. I

Prospero then buried deep in the earth his magical books and wand, for he was resolved never more to make use of the magic art. And having thus overcome his enemies, and being reconciled to his brother and the King of Naples, nothing now remained to complete his happiness, but to revisit his native land, to take possession of his dukedom, and to witness the happy nuptials[64] of his daughter and Prince Ferdinand, which the king said should be instantly celebrated with great splendour on their return to Naples.

At which place, under the safe convoy[65] of the spirit Ariel, they, after a pleasant voyage, soon arrived.

64 nuptials [ˈnʌpʃəlz] (n.) 婚禮
65 convoy [ˈkɑːnvɔɪ] (n.) 護送

Quotation
THE TEMPEST

Caliban   You taught me language, and my profit on it
              Is, I know how to curse. (I, ii, 363-364)

卡力班   你教我語言,而我從中獲得的
            就是,我學會怎麼詛咒。
            (第一幕,第二景,363-364 行)

Antonio   What's past is prologue; what to come,
              In yours and my discharge. (II, I, 253-254)

安東尼   過去的只是引子,以後要來的
            就是你和我的事了。
            (第二幕,第一景,253-254 行)

Prospero We are such stuff
As dreams are made on; and our little life
Is rounded with a sleep. (IV, i, 156-158)

普洛斯 我們就是
夢幻的原料；我們短暫的一生，
前後都環繞著酣睡。
（第四幕，第一景，156-158 行）

Miranda O wonder!
How many goodly creatures are there here!
How beauteous mankind is! O brave new world
That has such people in't! (V, i, 181-184)

米蘭達 哦，神奇。
外頭有多少善良的生物，
人類真是美麗！哦，美麗新世界。
裡頭竟有這樣的人兒！
（第五幕，第一景，181-184 行）

The Winter's Tale

冬天的故事

FLORIZEL AND PERDITA

導讀

陳敬旻

《冬天的故事》寫作年代略早於《暴風雨》，此兩劇同為「浪漫劇」（romance），又有離散重聚、失而復得的主題，照理說彼此具有密切關係，但在初版的莎士比亞全集《第一對開本》（the First Folio）裡，《暴風雨》是十四個喜劇裡的第一齣喜劇，《冬天的故事》卻是最後一齣。

浪漫劇的劇情

本劇的故事情節像是不合理的浪漫小說或童話故事，有時空的移轉、季節的交替和摧毀後的復原。全劇明顯劃分為兩大段，前半段敘述隆冬時節的西西里宮廷內，國王雷提斯（Leontes）認定王后荷麥妮（Hermione）與幼時即認識的好友波希米亞國王波利茲（Polixenes）有染，國王妒火中燒，造成了看似無可挽回的罪惡與悲傷。

後半段的故事發生於十六年之後，在春暖時光的波希米亞鄉間，遭到雷提斯狠心遺棄的女兒帕蒂坦（Perdita）初長成，在因緣際會下，和波利茲的獨子弗羅瑞（Florizel）共譜戀曲。但因為帕蒂坦出身低微，波利茲反對兩人結婚，兩人決定和忠臣卡密羅（Camillo）遠赴西西里。後來在雷提斯的宮裡，帕蒂坦真正的身分於此揭曉，王后荷麥妮也奇蹟似地復活，一家人最終和樂團圓。

嫉妒的愚昧

本劇故事源自略早於莎士比亞的劇作家葛林（Robert Greene）在 1588 年所著的小說《潘多托：時間致勝》（*Pandosto: The Triumph of Time*），此故事的主旨在表現嫉妒所招之惡果。《冬天的故事》前半段也具有相同意味。雷提斯懷疑猜忌，雷霆大怒，其內心的複雜糾葛，幾乎可與莎士比亞的悲劇角色相提並論。

雷提斯一如莎翁四大悲劇《奧賽羅》（*Othello*）中的奧賽羅，因嫉妒仇恨多年好友，間接害死愛妻，並失去王位繼承人的位置。《冬》劇強調的是因愚昧而自我摧殘的悲劇，主人翁必須因此長年忍受懊悔與孤獨。

Robert Greene (1558-1592)

荷麥妮是此劇中受苦最多、犧牲最大的角色。雷提斯亂吃飛醋，使她先後在公眾審判中遭到羞辱、失去心愛的兒子、與女兒分離，最後長期離群索居。劇中年幼的王子公主一死一棄，無辜受害。直到春季來臨，象徵新生與活力，年輕的一代才化悲為喜。

「時間」的概念

在前半部的故事裡，主人翁造成悲劇，後半部的故事就用時間和奇蹟來扳平悲劇。《冬》劇反映莎士比亞對「時間」的概念，他認為時間如水，能夠載舟亦能覆舟。時間能夠破壞亦能修復，它可以摧毀一切，也可以揭發真相。這種時間哲學和英國詩人史賓賽（Edmund Spenser, 1552-1599）的觀點相似，也因此可以得知，莎士比亞可能不僅知道史賓賽的作品，還進一步借用了他的概念。

荷麥妮在劇末奇蹟似地復生，令觀眾和讀者大吃一驚，人們以為她早已過世，一如葛林的小說《潘多托》。莎士比亞究竟是在最後一刻才改變心意，決定讓她復活，還是從開始就決定隱瞞觀眾，我們不得而知。但在戲劇史上，自始至終都將觀眾蒙在鼓裡的例子少之又少。

荷麥妮從雕像搖身一變成為真人，對現代的許多讀者和觀眾來說，根本是不可思議。然而在十七世紀初期的舞台上，這卻產生了極大的戲劇效果。荷麥妮解釋，雖然她早已原諒雷提斯，但一直到找回帕蒂坦才決定現身。這種說法顯示她之前活在遙遙無期的等待之中，強化了帕蒂坦出現的奇蹟性。

「天性」與「教養」

帕蒂坦出場時只是個牧羊女，卻因具有皇族血統而儀表出眾。莎士比亞在此又觸及了「自然天性」（nature）和「人為教養」（nurture）的主題。在此劇之後推出的《暴風雨》中，也談到了這個主題，並延續了「天性重於教養」的觀念。

戲劇的演出

《冬》劇與另一齣戲《忠誠的牧羊女》（*The Faithful Shepherdess*）之間，也有令人莞爾的對比。《忠誠的牧羊女》是由莎士比亞所屬的國王御前劇團（King's Men），在推出《冬》劇前一兩年所製作演出的戲碼，由莎士比亞的接班人弗萊徹（John Fletcher）執筆，但那次的演出大為失敗。

弗萊徹在《忠》劇出版時曾為文撰序，說明自己原本打算寫一齣悲喜劇，卻因為內容與觀眾的期望相悖而告失敗。觀眾想看到盛大節慶歡欣熱鬧的氣氛，也想看演員穿著牧羊袍，牽著牧羊犬在舞台上活動，說些引人發噱的笑話，但他的劇本裡卻沒有安排這些場景。《冬》劇則不然，剪羊毛大會一景就充滿了通俗歡樂的成分，一點也沒有讓觀眾失望。

違反戲劇的三一律

《冬天的故事》於 1623 年首次發行在
《第一對開本》中。伊麗莎白時代的占
星家賽門‧福曼（Simon Forman）在日
記中寫道，1611 年 5 月，他在環球劇場
觀看了《冬天的故事》，這是該劇演出的
最早記錄。

BENJAMIN JONSON (1572-1637)

這個劇本在詹姆士王朝時期的演出雖然
得到觀眾的肯定，但是嚴肅的批評家卻
對此劇大加撻伐。莎士比亞的好友英國
作家強生（Ben Jonson, 1572-1637）在
1631 年就說，《冬》劇之流——包括
《暴風雨》——顛覆所有的或然率和自然
法則，讓大自然也不得不畏懼。

十八世紀的英國作家強生（Samuel
Johnson, 1709-1784）則認為，《冬》劇
最大的缺陷在於中間一段長達十六年的
空白，違反了戲劇的「三一律」*。

SAMUEL JOHNSON (1709-1784)

* 所謂戲劇三一律，乃指：戲劇的故事情節，在時間上都發
　生在一天之內，地點都在同一個場影，劇情只有一條主
　線、一個主題。

寓言的意涵

現代的批評早已不作如此想，而是將焦點放在本劇的象徵性，甚至傾向於將此劇視為寓言。劇中人犯下大錯後獲得寬恕的架構，類似《一報還一報》（*Measure for Measure*），因此也有人認為這齣戲帶有基督教的訓示意味。

而前面曾提及過的占師家賽門·福曼，他在觀賞本劇後似乎很滿意。他巨細靡遺地描述該場表演的每個過程，他表示，劇情雖然十分複雜，卻沒有任何荒謬的場景和缺陷。或許有人會感到好奇，那隻把安提貢（Antigonus）拖出場外的熊，到底是真熊還是由演員假扮而成，因為當時的倫敦市內有溫馴的熊，也有凶猛的鬥熊。

時至今日，《冬天的故事》在舞台上的出現次數，雖然不如莎士比亞其他的悲劇或喜劇，卻往往有出乎預料的演出效果。而在莎翁的浪漫劇中，《冬》劇的曝光率則是僅次於《暴風雨》。

Leontes	雷提斯	西西里國王 （King of Sicily）
Hermione	荷麥妮	西西里國的王后
Polixenes	波利茲	波希米亞國王 （King of Bohemia）， 西西里國王雷提斯自 幼便認識的好友
Perdita	帕蒂坦	被父親雷提斯狠心遺 棄而流落在外的女兒
Florizel	弗羅瑞	波希米亞國王波利茲 的獨子，為追求帕蒂 坦，曾化名 Doricles （多里克）
Camillo	卡密羅	西西里國王雷提斯的 勳爵，是一位正直的 臣子

Mamillius	馬密利	西西里國王雷提斯的年幼兒子,不幸因憂傷而早逝
Paulina	寶琳娜	安提貢之妻,王后荷麥妮的密友
Antigonus	安提貢	西西里勳爵,執行遺棄帕蒂坦的任務後身亡
Emilia	愛蜜莉	在地牢服侍荷麥妮的侍女
Cleomenes & Dion	克里歐 & 迪翁	雷提斯派去德爾菲的阿波羅廟求神諭的使者

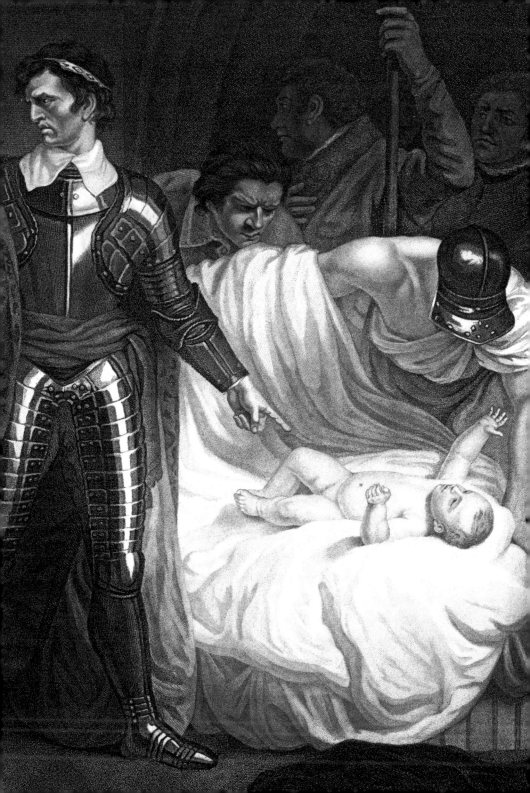

🎧 33 Leontes, King of Sicily and his queen, the beautiful and virtuous Hermione, once lived in the greatest harmony together. So happy was Leontes in the love of this excellent lady, that he had no wish ungratified, except that he sometimes desired to see again, and to present to his queen, his old companion and schoolfellow, Polixenes, King of Bohemia.

🎧 34 Leontes and Polixenes were brought up together from their infancy[1], but being, by the death of their fathers, called to reign over their respective kingdoms, they had not met for many years, though they frequently interchanged gifts, letters, and loving embassies.

At length, after repeated invitations, Polixenes came from Bohemia to the Sicilian court, to make his friend Leontes a visit.

At first this visit gave nothing but pleasure to Leontes. He recommended the friend of his youth to the queen's particular attention, and seemed in the presence of his dear friend and old companion to have his felicity[2] quite completed. They talked over old times; their school-days and their youthful pranks[3] were remembered, and recounted to Hermione, who always took a cheerful part in these conversations.

1 infancy [ˈɪnfənsi] (n.) 幼年時期
2 felicity [fɪˈlɪsɪti] (n.) 幸福
3 prank [præŋk] (n.) 惡作劇

When, after a long stay, Polixenes was preparing to depart, Hermione, at the desire of her husband, joined her entreaties[4] to his that Polixenes would prolong his visit.

And now began this good queen's sorrow; for Polixenes refusing to stay at the request of Leontes, was won over by Hermione's gentle and persuasive words to put off his departure for some weeks longer.

Upon this, although Leontes had so long known the integrity[5] and honourable principles of his friend Polixenes, as well as the excellent disposition[6] of his virtuous queen, he was seized with an ungovernable jealousy.

4 entreaty [ɪnˈtriːti] (n.) 〔正式〕懇求
5 integrity [ɪnˈtɛgrəti] (n.) 正直；誠實
6 disposition [ˌdɪspəˈzɪʃən] (n.) 性情；氣質

🎧 36   Every attention Hermione showed to Polixenes,
though by her husband's particular desire, and
merely to please him, increased the unfortunate
king's jealousy; and from being a loving and a true
friend, and the best and fondest of husbands, Leontes
became suddenly a savage and inhuman monster.
Sending for Camillo, one of the lords of his court,
and telling him of the suspicion he entertained[7], he
commanded him to poison Polixenes.

Camillo was a good man; and he, well knowing
that the jealousy of Leontes had not the slightest
foundation in truth, instead of poisoning Polixenes,
acquainted him with the king his master's orders,
and agreed to escape with him out of the Sicilian
dominions; and Polixenes, with the assistance of
Camillo, arrived safe in his own kingdom of Bohemia,
where Camillo lived from that time in the king's
court, and became the chief friend and favourite of
Polixenes.

[7] entertain [ˌentərˈteɪn] (v.) 準備考慮

Leontes.   Might'st bespice a cup,
To give mine enemy a lasting wink;
Which draught to me were cordial.
    Camillo.   Sir, my lord.   *Act I. Scene II.*

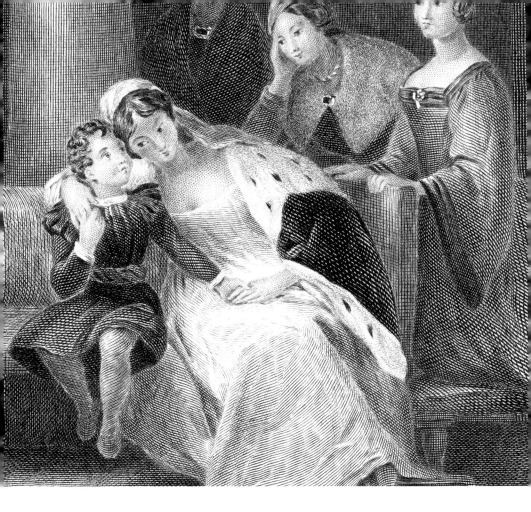

  The flight of Polixenes enraged[8] the jealous Leontes still more; he went to the queen's apartment, where the good lady was sitting with her little son Mamillius, who was just beginning to tell one of his best stories to amuse his mother, when the king entered, and taking the child away, sent Hermione to prison.

8 enrage [ɪnˈreɪdʒ] (v.) 激怒

Hamilton del.

Starling sc.

WINTER'S TALE

Leontes, Hermione, Mamillius &c.

Act II. Scene I.

🎧38   Mamillius, though but a very young child, loved his mother tenderly; and when he saw her so dishonoured, and found she was taken from him to be put into a prison, he took it deeply to heart, and drooped[9] and pined[10] away by slow degrees, losing his appetite and his sleep, till it was thought his grief would kill him.

9 droop [druːp] (v.) 頹喪；委靡不振
10 pine [paɪn] (v.) 消瘦；憔悴

The king, when he had sent his queen to prison, commanded Cleomenes and Dion, two Sicilian lords, to go to Delphos, there to inquire of the oracle[11] at the temple of Apollo, if his queen had been unfaithful to him.

When Hermione had been a short time in prison, she was brought to bed of a daughter; and the poor lady received much comfort from the sight of her pretty baby, and she said to it: "My poor little prisoner, I am as innocent as you are."

Hermione had a kind friend in the noble-spirited Paulina, who was the wife of Antigonus, a Sicilian lord and when the lady Paulina heard her royal mistress was brought to bed, she went to the prison where Hermione was confined; and she said to Emilia, a lady who attended upon Hermione, "I pray you, Emilia, tell the good queen, if her majesty dare trust me with her little babe, I will carry it to the king, its father; we do not know how he may soften at the sight of his innocent child."

11 oracle [ˈɔːrəkəl] (n.) 神諭

"Most worthy madam," replied Emilia, "I will acquaint the queen with your noble offer; she was wishing today that she had any friend who would venture to present the child to the king."

"And tell her," said Paulina, "that I will speak boldly to Leontes in her defence."

"May you be for ever blessed," said Emilia, "for your kindness to our gracious queen!"

Emilia then went to Hermione, who joyfully gave up her baby to the care of Paulina, for she had feared that no one would dare venture to present the child to its father.

Paulina took the newborn infant, and forcing herself into the king's presence, notwithstanding her husband, fearing the king's anger, endeavoured to prevent her, she laid the babe at its father's feet, and Paulina made a noble speech to the king in defence of Hermione, and she reproached[12] him severely for his inhumanity, and implored him to have mercy on his innocent wife and child.

12 reproach [rɪˈproʊtʃ] (v.) 責備

Paulina. Here 'tis; commends it to your blessing.

Leontes. Out!

A mankind witch! Hence with her out o' door.

Act II. Scene III.

But Paulina's spirited remonstrances[13] only aggravated[14] Leontes' displeasure, and he ordered her husband Antigonus to take her from his presence.

When Paulina went away, she left the little baby at its father's feet, thinking when he was alone with it, he would look upon it, and have pity on its helpless innocence.

The good Paulina was mistaken: for no sooner was she gone than the merciless father ordered Antigonus, Paulina's husband, to take the child, and carry it out to sea, and leave it upon some desert shore to perish.

Antigonus, unlike the good Camillo, too well obeyed the orders of Leontes; for he immediately carried the child on shipboard, and put out to sea, intending to leave it on the first desert coast he could find.

13 remonstrance [rɪˈmɑːnstrəns] (n.) 抗議
14 aggravate [ˈæɡrəveɪt] (v.) 使惡化

Delos

 So firmly was the king persuaded of the guilt of
Hermione, that he would not wait for the return of
Cleomenes and Dion, whom he had sent to consult
the oracle of Apollo at Delphos, but before the queen
was recovered from her lying-in[15], and from her grief
for the loss of her precious baby, he had her brought
to a public trial before all the lords and nobles of his
court.

15 lying-in (n.) 分娩

And when all the great lords, the judges, and all
the nobility of the land were assembled together
to try Hermione, and that unhappy queen was
standing as a prisoner before her subjects[16] to receive
their judgement Cleomenes and Dion entered the
assembly, and presented to the king the answer of the
oracle, sealed up; and Leontes commanded the seal
to be broken, and the words of the oracle to be read
aloud, and these were the words:

"Hermione is innocent,
Polixenes blameless,
Camillo a true subject,
Leontes a jealous tyrant,
and the king shall live without an heir
if that which is lost be not found."

16 subject ['sʌbdʒɪkt] (n.) 庶民；子民

🎧 44   The king would give no credit to the words of the oracle: he said it was a falsehood invented by the queen's friends, and he desired the judge to proceed in the trial of the queen; but while Leontes was speaking, a man entered and told him that the Prince Mamillius, hearing his mother was to be tried for her life, struck with grief and shame, had suddenly died.

  Hermione, upon hearing of the death of this dear affectionate[17] child, who had lost his life in sorrowing for her misfortune, fainted; and Leontes, pierced[18] to the heart by the news, began to feel pity for his unhappy queen, and he ordered Paulina, and the ladies who were her attendants, to take her away, and use means for her recovery.

  Paulina soon returned, and told the king that Hermione was dead.

[17] affectionate [əˈfekʃənət] (a.) 摯愛的
[18] pierce [pɪrs] (v.) 深深地打動

🎧45 　When Leontes heard that the queen was dead, he repented of his cruelty to her; and now that he thought his ill-usage had broken Hermione's heart, he believed her innocent; and now he thought the words of the oracle were true, as he knew "if that which was lost was not found," which he concluded was his young daughter, he should be without an heir, the young Prince Mamillius being dead; and he would give his kingdom now to recover his lost daughter: and Leontes gave himself up to remorse[19], and passed many years in mournful thoughts and repentant grief.

　The ship in which Antigonus carried the infant princess out to sea was driven by a storm upon the coast of Bohemia, the very kingdom of the good King Polixenes. Here Antigonus landed, and here he left the little baby.

19 remorse [rɪˈmɔːrs] (n.) 懊悔；悔恨

WINTER'S TALE
Antigonus pursued by a Bear.
Act III. Scene III.

Wright del.

Starling sc.

🎧46　　Antigonus never returned to Sicily to tell Leontes where he had left his daughter, for as he was going back to the ship, a bear came out of the woods, and tore him to pieces; a just punishment on him for obeying the wicked order of Leontes.

The child was dressed in rich clothes and jewels; for Hermione had made it very fine when she sent it to Leontes, and Antigonus had pinned a paper to its mantle[20], and the name of *Perdita* written thereon, and words obscurely intimating[21] its high birth and untoward[22] fate.

20 mantle ['mæntl] (n.) 斗篷
21 intimate ['ɪntəmət] (v.) 提示；暗示
22 untoward [ˌʌn'tɔːrd] (a.) 不幸的

This poor deserted baby was found by a shepherd. He was a humane man, and so he carried the little Perdita home to his wife, who nursed it tenderly; but poverty tempted[23] the shepherd to conceal[24] the rich prize he had found: therefore he left that part of the country, that no one might know where he got his riches, and with part of Perdita's jewels he bought herds of sheep, and became a wealthy shepherd.

He brought up Perdita as his own child, and she knew not she was any other than a shepherd's daughter.

23 tempt ['tempt] (v.) 誘惑
24 conceal [kən'siːl] (v.) 隱藏；隱瞞

The little Perdita grew up a lovely maiden; and though she had no better education than that of a shepherd's daughter, yet so did the natural graces she inherited from her royal mother shine forth in her untutored mind, that no one from her behaviour would have known she had not been brought up in her father's court.

Polixenes, the King of Bohemia, had an only son, whose name was Florizel. As this young prince was hunting near the shepherd's dwelling, he saw the old man's supposed daughter; and the beauty, modesty, and queen-like deportment[25] of Perdita caused him instantly to fall in love with her.

25 deportment [dɪ'pɔːrtmənt] (n.) 行為；舉止

🎧 49 He soon, under the name of Doricles, and in the disguise of a private gentleman, became a constant visitor at the old shepherd's house. Florizel's frequent absences from court alarmed Polixenes; and setting people to watch his son, he discovered his love for the shepherd's fair daughter.

Polixenes then called for Camillo, the faithful Camillo, who had preserved his life from the fury of Leontes, and desired that he would accompany him to the house of the shepherd, the supposed father of Perdita.

Hamilton del   Starhng sc

WINTER'S TALE

Florizel, Perdita, Polixenes &c.

Act IV Scene III

50 Polixenes and Camillo, both in disguise, arrived at the old shepherd's dwelling while they were celebrating the feast of sheepshearing; and though they were strangers, yet at the sheepshearing every guest being made welcome, they were invited to walk in, and join in the general festivity.

Nothing but mirth[26] and jollity[27] was going forward. Tables were spread, and great preparations were making for the rustic feast. Some lads and lasses were dancing on the green before the house, while others of the young men were buying ribands[28], gloves, and such toys, of a pedlar at the door.

26 mirth [mɜːrθ] (n.) 歡樂
27 jollity ['dʒɑːlɪti] (n.) 愉快
28 riband ['rɪbənd] (n.)〔古〕飾帶（同 ribbon）

Autolycus. Lawn as white as driven snow ;
Cyprus black as e'er was crow.

Act IV. Scene III.

While this busy scene was going forward, Florizel and Perdita sat quietly in a retired corner, seemingly more pleased with the conversation of each other, than desirous of engaging in the sports and silly amusements of those around them.

The king was so disguised that it was impossible his son could know him: he therefore advanced near enough to hear the conversation. The simple yet elegant manner in which Perdita conversed with his son did not a little surprise Polixenes: he said to Camillo: "This is the prettiest low-born lass I ever saw; nothing she does or says but looks like something greater than herself, too noble for this place."

Camillo replied: "Indeed she is the very queen of curds[29] and cream."

"Pray, my good friend," said the king to the old shepherd," what fair swain[30] is that talking with your daughter?"

"They call him Doricles," replied the shepherd. "He says he loves my daughter; and, to speak truth, there is not a kiss to choose which loves the other best. If young Doricles can get her, she shall bring him that he little dreams of"; meaning the remainder of Perdita's jewels; which, after he had bought herds of sheep with part of them, he had carefully hoarded up for her marriage portion.

29 curd [kɜːrd] (n.) 凝乳（牛奶變酸時的凝結物，可用來製作乳酪）
30 swain [sweɪn] (n.) 戀愛中的青年（特指仰慕者或情人）

Polixenes then addressed his son. "How now, young man!" said he: "your heart seems full of something that takes off your mind from feasting. When I was young, I used to load my love with presents; but you have let the pedlar go and have bought your lass no toy."

The young prince, who little thought he was talking to the king his father, replied, "Old sir, she prizes not such trifles; the gifts which Perdita expects from me are locked up in my heart."

Then turning to Perdita, he said to her, "O hear me, Perdita, before this ancient gentleman, who it seems was once himself a lover; he shall hear what I profess."

Perdita.   These are flowers
Of middle summer, and, I think, they are given
To men of middle age. You are very welcome.   *Act IV. Scene III.*

🎧 54 Florizel then called upon the old stranger to be a witness to a solemn promise of marriage which he made to Perdita, saying to Polixenes, "I pray you, mark our contract."

"Mark your divorce, young sir," said the king, discovering himself.

Téli rege

Polixenes then reproached his son for daring to contract himself to this low-born maiden, calling Perdita "shepherd's brat[31], sheep-hook," and other disrespectful names; and threatening, if ever she suffered his son to see her again, he would put her, and the old shepherd her father, to a cruel death.

The king then left them in great wrath[32], and ordered Camillo to follow him with Prince Florizel.

When the king had departed, Perdita, whose royal nature was roused by Polixenes' reproaches, said, "Though we are all undone, I was not much afraid; and once or twice I was about to speak, and tell him plainly that the selfsame sun which shines upon his palace, hides not his face from our cottage, but looks on both alike."

31 brat [bræt] (n.) 〔貶〕小兒
32 wrath [ræθ] (n.) 〔文〕盛怒

Then sorrowfully she said: "But now I am awakened from this dream, I will queen it no further. Leave me, sir; I will go milk my ewes[33] and weep."

The kind-hearted Camillo was charmed with the spirit and propriety[34] of Perdita's behaviour; and perceiving that the young prince was too deeply in love to give up his mistress at the command of his royal father, he thought of a way to befriend the lovers, and at the same time to execute a favourite scheme he had in his mind.

Camillo had long known that Leontes, the King of Sicily, was become a true penitent[35]; and though Camillo was now the favoured friend of King Polixenes, he could not help wishing once more to see his late royal master and his native home. He therefore proposed to Florizel and Perdita that they should accompany him to the Sicilian court, where he would engage Leontes should protect them till, through his mediation, they could obtain pardon from Polixenes, and his consent to their marriage.

---

33 ewe [juː] (n.) 母羊
34 propriety [prə'praɪəti] (n.) 〔正式〕行為得體；禮貌
35 penitent ['penɪtənt] (n.) 悔過者

To this proposal they joyfully agreed; and Camillo, who conducted everything relative to their flight[36], allowed the old shepherd to go along with them.

The shepherd took with him the remainder of Perdita's jewels, her baby clothes, and the paper which he had found pinned to her mantle.

After a prosperous voyage, Florizel and Perdita, Camillo and the old shepherd, arrived in safety at the court of Leontes. Leontes, who still mourned his dead Hermione and his lost child, received Camillo with great kindness, and gave a cordial[37] welcome to Prince Florizel.

But Perdita, whom Florizel introduced as his princess, seemed to engross[38] all Leontes' attention: perceiving a resemblance between her and his dead queen Hermione, his grief broke out afresh, and he said, such a lovely creature might his own daughter have been, if he had not so cruelly destroyed her.

---

36 flight [flaɪt] (n.) 逃亡
37 cordial [ˈkɔːrdʒəl] (a.) 衷心的；真摯的
38 engross [ɪnˈɡroʊs] (v.) 使全神貫注

"And then, too," said he to Florizel, "I lost the society and friendship of your grave father, whom I now desire more than my life once again to look upon."

When the old shepherd heard how much notice the king had taken of Perdita, and that he had lost a daughter, who was exposed in infancy, he fell to comparing the time when he found the little Perdita, with the manner of its exposure, the jewels and other tokens of its high birth; from all which it was impossible for him not to conclude that Perdita and the king's lost daughter were the same.

Florizel and Perdita, Camillo and the faithful Paulina, were present when the old shepherd related to the king the manner in which he had found the child, and also the circumstance of Antigonus' death, he having seen the bear seize upon him.

🎧 59 He showed the rich mantle in which Paulina
remembered Hermione had wrapped the child;
and he produced a jewel which she remembered
Hermione had tied about Perdita's neck, and he gave
up the paper which Paulina knew to be the writing of
her husband; it could not be doubted that Perdita was
Leontes' own daughter: but oh! the noble struggles of
Paulina, between sorrow for her husband's death, and
joy that the oracle was fulfilled, in the king's heir, his
long-lost daughter being found.

When Leontes heard that Perdita was his daughter,
the great sorrow that he felt that Hermione was not
living to behold[39] her child, made him that he could
say nothing for a long time, but "O thy mother, thy
mother!"

39 behold [bɪˈhoʊld] (v.)〔舊〕〔文〕看見;看

🎧60 Paulina interrupted this joyful yet distressful scene, with saying to Leontes, that she had a statue newly finished by that rare Italian master, Julio Romano, which was such a perfect resemblance of the queen, that would his majesty be pleased to go to her house and look upon it, he would be almost ready to think it was Hermione herself. Thither[40] then they all went; the king anxious to see the semblance of his Hermione, and Perdita longing to behold what the mother she never saw did look like.

40 thither [ˈθɪðər] (adv.) 到彼處

🎧 61 When Paulina drew back the curtain which concealed this famous statue, so perfectly did it resemble Hermione, that all the king's sorrow was renewed at the sight: for a long time he had no power to speak or move.

"I like your silence, my liege[41]," said Paulina, "it the more shows your wonder. Is not this statue very like your queen?"

At length the king said: "O, thus she stood, even with such majesty, when I first wooed her. But yet, Paulina, Hermione was not so aged as this statue looks."

Paulina replied: "So much the more the carver's excellence, who has made the statue as Hermione would have looked had she been living now. But let me draw the curtain, sire[42], lest presently you think it moves."

The king then said: "Do not draw the curtain, Would I were dead! See, Camillo, would you not think it breathed? Her eye seems to have motion in it."

41 liege [liːdʒ] (n.) 君主；王侯
42 sire [saɪr] (n.) 〔舊〕對國王或皇帝的敬稱

Hamilton del.   Starling ac.

🎧62 "I must draw the curtain, my liege," said Paulina.

"You are so transported[43], you will persuade yourself the statue lives."

"O, sweet Paulina," said Leontes, "make me think so twenty years together! Still methinks[44] there is an air comes from her. What fine chisel[45] could ever yet cut breath? Let no man mock me, for I will kiss her."

43 transport ['trænspɔːrt] (v.)〔文〕使忘我，使激動
44 methinks [mɪ'θɪŋks] (v.)〔古〕據我看來
45 chisel ['tʃɪzəl] (n.) 鑿子

Mrs WARNER as HERMIONE.

WINTER'S TALE
ACT 5 SCENE 3.

From a Daguerotype by Paine of Islington.

THE LONDON PRINTING AND PUBLISHING COMPANY

63

"Good my lord, forbear[46]!" said Paulina. "The ruddiness upon her lip is wet; you will stain your own with oily painting. Shall I draw the curtain?"

"No, not these twenty years," said Leontes.

Perdita, who all this time had been kneeling, and beholding in silent admiration the statue of her matchless mother, said now, "And so long could I stay here, looking upon my dear mother."

"Either forbear this transport," said Paulina to Leontes, "and let me draw the curtain; or prepare yourself for more amazement. I can make the statue move indeed; ay, and descend from off the pedestal[47], and take you by the hand. But then you will think, which I protest I am not, that I am assisted by some wicked powers."

"What you can make her do," said the astonished king, "I am content to look upon. What you can make her speak, I am content to hear; for it is as easy to make her speak as move."

---

46 forbear ['fɔːrber] (v.) 〔正式〕自制；忍耐
47 pedestal ['pedɪstəl] (n.) 臺座；塑像的墊座

WINTERS TALE.

——— Upon perceive, the Stars
shout not;

Act 5   Scene 3

Paulina then ordered some slow and solemn music, which she had prepared for the purpose, to strike up; and, to the amazement of all the beholders, the statue came down from off the pedestal, and threw its arms around Leontes' neck. The statue then began to speak, praying for blessings on her husband, and on her child, the newly-found Perdita.

No wonder that the statue hung upon Leontes' neck, and blessed her husband and her child. No wonder; for the statue was indeed Hermione herself, the real, the living queen.

Paulina had falsely reported to the king the death of Hermione, thinking that the only means to preserve her royal mistress' life; and with the good Paulina, Hermione had lived ever since, never choosing Leontes should know she was living, till she heard Perdita was found; for though she had long forgiven the injuries which Leontes had done to herself, she could not pardon his cruelty to his infant daughter.

His dead queen thus restored to life, his lost daughter found, the long-sorrowing Leontes could scarcely support the excess of his own happiness.

Nothing but congratulations and affectionate speeches were heard on all sides. Now the delighted parents thanked Prince Florizel for loving their lowlyseeming daughter; and now they blessed the good old shepherd for preserving their child. Greatly did Camillo and Paulina rejoice that they had lived to see so good an end of all their faithful services.

And as if nothing should be wanting to complete this strange and unlooked-for joy, King Polixenes himself now entered the palace.

When Polixenes first missed his son and Camillo, knowing that Camillo had long wished to return to Sicily, he conjectured[48] he should find the fugitives[49] here; and, following them with all speed, he happened to just arrive at this, the happiest moment of Leontes' life.

---

[48] conjecture [kənˈdʒektʃər] (v.) 猜測；推測
[49] fugitive [ˈfjuːdʒɪtɪv] (n.) 逃亡者；逃犯

🎧 66 Polixenes took a part in the general joy; he forgave his friend Leontes the unjust jealousy he had conceived against him, and they once more loved each other with all the warmth of their first boyish friendship. And there was no fear that Polixenes would now oppose his son's marriage with Perdita. She was no "sheep-hook" now, but the heiress of the crown of Sicily.

Thus have we seen the patient virtues of the long-suffering Hermione rewarded. That excellent lady lived many years with her Leontes and her Perdita, the happiest of mothers and of queens.

Polixenes　We were as twinn'd lambs that did frisk i'the sun,
And bleat the one at the other: what we chang'd
Was innocence for innocence; we knew not
The doctrine of ill-doing, no, nor dream'd
That any did. (Act 1, scene 2, lines 67-71)

波利茲　　　我們猶如在陽光下歡躍的一對孿生羔羊，
彼此交換著咩咩的叫喚：
我們以一片天真，與對方相待，
我們不懂得作惡，
也不曾想過人世間裡會有人行惡事。

（第一幕，第二景，67-71 行）

Shepherd　I think there is not half a kiss to choose
Who loves another best. (IV, iii, 175-176)

牧羊人　　　我想沒有半個吻能看得出誰愛誰多。

（第四幕，第三景，175-176 行）

Perdita　　The selfsame sun that shines upon his court
　　　　　　Hides not his visage from our cottage, but
　　　　　　Looks on alike. (IV, iii, 448-50)

帕蒂坦　　照耀他的皇宮的那個太陽，
　　　　　不對我們的村莊隱其光芒，而是
　　　　　一視同仁。

（第四幕，第三景，448-50 行）

國家圖書館出版品預行編目資料

悅讀莎士比亞故事 . 7, 暴風雨 & 冬天的故事 / Charles
and Mary Lamb 著;Cosmos Language Workshop 譯 .
-- 初版 . -- [臺北市]:寂天文化,
2011.07 面;公分 .

ISBN 978-986-184-891-4 (25K 平裝附光碟片)

1. 英語 2. 讀本

805.18   100011774

作者	Charles and Mary Lamb
譯者	Cosmos Language Workshop
編輯	歐寶妮
主編	黃鈺云
內文排版	謝青秀
製程管理	林欣穎
出版者	寂天文化事業股份有限公司
電話	02-2365-9739
傳真	02-2365-9835
網址	www.icosmos.com.tw
讀者服務	onlineservice@icosmos.com.tw
出版日期	2011 年 7 月 初版一刷（250101）
	版權所有 請勿翻印
郵撥帳號	1998620-0 寂天文化事業股份有限公司
	訂購金額 600(含) 元以上郵資免費
	訂購金額 600 元以下者,請外加郵資 60 元
	〔若有破損,請寄回更換,謝謝。〕

CONTENTS

《暴風雨》Practice 2

Practice Answers 8

《冬天的故事》Practice 9

Practice Answers 14

《暴風雨》中譯...... 15

《冬天的故事》中譯...... 24

1 Postreading

What would you do if you had the power of magic?

2 Vocabulary

A. Fill in the blanks with the words from the following list.

advocate	altered	compelling
grumbling	implored	lamenting
stupefied	famished	prosperous
recollection		

1. Ariel had the charge of _____ Caliban to these services.

2. I have done you worthy service, told you no lies, made no mistakes, served you without grudge or _____.

3. What! An _____ for an impostor!

4. When fatigued with wandering about, and _____ for want of food, he had suddenly set before them a delicious banquet.

5. Grief and terror had so _____ their senses, that they did not know Prospero.

6. Give me leave to attend your ship home with _____ gales.

B. Read the sentences and write a synonym of the underlined words.

1. _____ It seems to me like the <u>recollection</u> of a dream. But had I not once four or five women who attended upon me?

2. _____ He is safe in a corner of the isle, sitting with his arms folded, sadly <u>lamenting</u> the loss of the king, his father, whom he concludes drowned.

3. _____ He is somewhat <u>altered</u> by grief, or you might call him a handsome person.

4. _____ Antonio with tears, and sad words of sorrow and true repentance, <u>implored</u> his brother's forgiveness.

3 Identification

A. Who are they? Fill in the blanks with the characters from the following list.

Antonio	Ariel	Caliban
Ferdinand	Gonzalo	King of Naples
Miranda	Prospero	Syncorax

1. _____ A witch, who died before Prospero's arrival, had enchanted the island and imprisoned many good spirits in the bodies of large trees.

2. _____ An ugly monster, and son of the witch, whom Prospero employed like a slave.

3. _____ Chief of these gentle spirits who were obedient to the will of Prospero.

4. _____ A very beautiful young lady who came to an island so young, that she had no memory of having seen any other human face than her father's.

5. _____ Duke of Milan, who deprived of his dukedom, landed on an island with his daughter.

6. _____ Son of the King of Naples, who fell in love with Miranda at the first sight.

B. Who said or did these?

1. _____ "Be not so amazed; there is no harm done. I have so ordered it, that no person in the ship shall receive any hurt.

2. _____ "I will soon move you. You must be brought, I find, for the Lady Miranda to have a sight of your pretty person. Come, sir, follow me.

3. _____ "My affections are most humble. I have no wish to see a goodlier man.

3

4. _____ "O wonder! what noble creatures these are! It must surely be a brave world that has such people in it.

5. _____ "She seems the goddess that has parted us, and brought us thus together.

6. _____ Who was the kind lord who had privately placed in the boat water, provisions, apparel, and some books which Prospero prized above his dukedom?

---

4 **Comprehension: Choose the correct answer.**

___ 1. What was the study of which Prospero had a good knowledge?
   a) Geometry. b) Geography. c) Magic. d) Astrology.

___ 2. Why were the gentle spirits obedient to the will of Prospero?
   a) Because he imprisoned them in the bodies of large trees.
   b) Because he released them from the bodies of large trees.
   c) Because he took Caliban to his cell and taught him to speak.
   d) Because he raised a dreadful sea storm.

___ 3. Why did Antonio deprive Prospero of his dukedom?
   a) Prospero was ignorant of who he was or where he came from.
   b) Prospero dedicated his whole time to the bettering of his mind and neglected all the state affairs.
   c) Prospero had always been heard holding conversation with the empty air.
   d) Prospero gave him the opportunity to be popular among the subjects, which awakened in his bad nature a proud ambition.

___ 4. What was Prospero's reason to raise the violent tempest?
   a) To cast the King of Naples and Antonio ashore upon the island.
   b) To show Miranda his useful magic.
   c) To preserve Miranda's life.
   d) To make Ariel perform his faithful charge.

____ 5. How did Prospero try Ferdinand's constancy?
a) To study magic with him.
b) To give a speech of his love for her.
c) To teach Caliban to speak.
d) To pile up some heavy logs of wood.

____ 6. The train was brought to Prospero's presence by the wild music Ariel played. Which of the following statements of this scene was not true?
a) Prospero chided them and would not forgive them.
b) They did not know Prospero because of grief and terror.
c) Antonio with tears, and sad words of sorrow and true repentance, implored his brother's forgiveness.
d) King of Naples expressed his sincere remorse for having assisted Antonio to depose his brother.

____ 7. What was the gift Prospero had in store for King of Naples?
a) Ferdinand sitting with his arms folded in a corner of the isle.
b) Ferdinand carrying the logs with the help of Miranda.
c) Ferdinand playing chess with Miranda.
d) Ferdinand holding Miranda's hands in the happy nuptials.

____ 8. Which of the following did Ariel not do?
a) Coming slily and pinching Caliban, and tumbling him down in the mire.
b) Gently touching Miranda with a magic wand to make her fall fast asleep.
c) Leading Ferdinand to Prospero and Miranda with his voice.
d) Appearing visible before Gonzalo, Antonio and King of Naples in the shape of a harpy.

5 Discussion

1. How did Prospero, as an outsider of the island, control the aboriginal creatures such as Ariel and Caliban? Was it a good or a bad control? Were they content to obey him? What would have happened if Prospero had never landed the island? Think also about his control over Miranda. He made her fall in

love with Ferdinand, so that she could be Queen of Naples when Ferdinand came to the throne. Was it a good or a bad control?

2. Do you think that Miranda would still have loved Ferdinand if she had had not lived on that island and had seen other men? Why or why not?

3. *The Tempest* was the last play written by Shakespeare. Some critics regard the protagonist Prospero as Shakespeare's self-projection, and that the tempest and other magic he commanded as the plays Shakespeare had written. When Prospero buried his magic books deep in the earth, it meant that Shakespeare would stop playwriting. What do you think of this interpretation? Does it make sense? Can you prove its validity?

---

6 | What's in the Magic Book?

Prospero has many books on the art of magic. It was with the help of those books that he could command the creatures on the island and raise the harmless tempest. Imagine what magic is taught in the magic book. Write "Table of Contents" of the book or instructions for some particular magic skills.

---

7 | Stage the Story Another Point of View

There are many theatrical elements in *The Tempest*—the flying Ariel, the deformed Caliban, the magic, the strange island, etc. Why don't we put on a production of it? But how would you like to present *The Tempest* if you stage the play? Consider the following aspects:

1. Who would play Ariel and Caliban? Are they males or females? Big or small? Any particular figures? What would their voices, gestures, movements, or costume/make up be like?
2. What does the island look like? How do you shape the "cell" and the "large trees"? Any creative ideas for the visual scenery of this island that has no other inhabitants?
3. How to do the tempest scene? Would you add some sound effects to it? Would you present it with the aid of technology such as slides, film, large computer screens and speakers?

8　Points of View

Choose one of the following characters and write a monologue from his or her point of view on what kind of a person Prospero is. State both the positive and negative sides.

> *Miranda*
>
> *Ariel*
>
> *Caliban*
>
> *Antonio*
>
> *Gonzalo*
>
> *Ferdinand*

《暴風雨》Answers

2 Vocabulary
A.

1. compelling
2. grumbling
3. advocate
4. famished
5. stupefied
6. prosperous

3 Identification
A.

1. Syncorax
2. Caliban
3. Ariel
4. Miranda
5. Prospero
6. Ferdinand

B.

1. Prospero
2. Ariel
3. Miranda
4. Miranda
5. King of Naples
6. Gonzalo

4 Comprehension

1. c
2. b
3. d
4. a
5. d
6. a
7. c
8. b

《冬天的故事》Practice

I Postreading

1. What do you think about jealousy?

2. Are you for or against love between different social levels?

2 Vocabulary

A. Fill in the blanks with the words from the following list.

engross	integrity	pierced
rejoice	scarcely	

1. Leontes had so long known the_____ and honourable principles of his friend Polixenes.

2. Leontes, _____ to the heart by the news, began to feel pity for his unhappy queen.

3. Perdita seemed to _____ all Leontes' attention.

4. Leontes could _____ support the excess of his own happiness.

5. Greatly did Camillo and Paulina _____ that they had lived to see so good an end of all their faithful services.

B. Make your own sentences with these words followed by their meanings.

1. conceal: (v.) hide, keep secret

_____

2. reward: (n.) to give a recompense for service or merit

_____

3. tempt: (v.) attract (somebody) to have or do something

_____

4. venture: (v.) undertaking in which there's risk

_____

5. wrath: (n.) (liter) great anger; indignation

_____

A. Draw a diagram to show the relations of these characters.

Antigonus	Camillo	Florizel	the shepherd
Hermione	Leontes	Mamillius	Polixenes
Paulina	Perdita		

B. Who said or did these? Choose from the above list.

1. _____ "This is the prettiest low-born lass I ever saw; nothing she does or says but looks like something greater than herself, too noble for this place."

2. _____ "To speak truth, there is not a kiss to choose which loves the other best."

3. _____ "She prizes not such trifles; the gifts which Perdita expects from me are locked up in my heart."

4. _____ "The selfsame sun which shines upon his palace, hides not his face from our cottage, but looks on both alike."

5. _____ "Still methinks there is an air comes from her. What fine chisel could ever yet cut breath? Let no man mock me, for I will kiss her."

6. _____ "I can make the statue move indeed; ay, and descend from off the pedestal, and take you by the hand."

7. _____ Who was killed by a bear after he had pinned a paper to the baby's mantle, and the name of _Perdita_ written thereon, and carried the infant princess out to sea?

8. _____ Who thought of a way to befriend Florizel and Perdita, and at the same time to execute his favourite scheme?

Comprehension: Choose the correct answer.

____1. Leontes was so happy in the love of this excellent lady, that he had no wish ungratified, except that he sometimes desired to:
   a) Have a princess to complete the felicity of his royal family.
   b) See again, and to present to his queen, his old companion and schoolfellow, Polixenes.
   c) Send his Sicilian lords to inquire of the oracle at the temple of Apollo, if his country would grow stronger.
   d) Request Julio Romano, the Italian master, to carve a statue for his queen.

____ 2. What began the good queen's sorrow?
   a) Leontes was seized with an ungovernable jealousy.
   b) Mamillius drooped and pined away by slow degrees, losing his appetite and his sleep.
   c) Her daughter was carried out to sea and was left upon some desert shore to perish.
   d) The words of the oracles said that she was unfaithful to Leontes.

____ 3. Why did Paulina leave the little baby at its Leontes' feet when she was taken away?
   a) She forgot to take it along with her in a haste.
   b) She didn't persuade Leontes and was ashamed to take it back to Hermione.
   c) She thought that when he was alone with it, he would look upon it, and have pity on its helpless innocence.
   d) She disliked it and intended to leave it to the furious king's cruel hands.

____ 4. Which of the following was not in the oracle?
   a) Hermione is innocent.
   b) Polixenes blameless.
   c) Camillo a true subject.
   d) Leontes a true penitent.

____ 5. Why did Polixenes object to Florizel and Perdita's marriage?
   a) She was a low-born maiden.
   b) Polixenes also conceived love for her.
   c) Camillo advised him not to consent on this marriage.

11

d) Polixenes had an unpleasant conversion with the shepherd.

___ 6. Which of the following did not help the shepherd and Leontes to conclude that Perdita was the king's lost daughter?
a) The manner of its exposure.
b) The paper of Antigonus' writing.
c) The jewels and rich mantle.
d) Perdita's inherited natural graces.

___ 7. What was Polixenes' intent of coming to Sicily for the second time?
a) To take a part in the happiest moment in Leontes' life.
b) To persuade Camillo to go back to Bohemia with him.
c) To revenge on Leontes for the unjust jealousy he had conceived against him.
d) To find the fugitives-Florizel and Perdita.

___ 8. The excess of Leontes' happiness did not include:
a) His lost daughter has found.
b) His dead queen has restored to life.
c) His son has come back to life.
d) Polixenes forgave his unjust jealousy.

5 Discussion

1. Though Leontes was jealous of Polixenes, this old friend's stay in Sicily was never long enough to produce a baby. Why do you think that Leontes would desire to have his own baby perished?

2. Which influences a person more, nature or nurture? Perdita was sent away not long after her birth. What were the royal qualities she inherited from Hermione and Polixenes that could outdo the personality she had formed during the untutored years she spent night and day with her shepherd father?

6

Another Point of View

1. You are Perdita, and you never doubt that you are a country maid. All of a sudden, you realized that your father is a king and Florizel is a prince. What would you react to all this? What about the parents you' ve lived with all your life?

2. You are Polixenes. What would be on your mind when you headed for Sicily? What would you think of your past with Leontes? Would you still reconcile with him if you did not find Florizel and Perdita there?

7

Challenge

Imagine how the daily lives Hermione had spent the years with Paulina ware about. What was her funeral like? How could she have been undiscovered? Did the maids know that she was alive? Had she never been out of the palace? etc.

《冬天的故事》 Answers

2 Vocabulary
A.

1. integrity
2. pierced
3. engross
4. scarcely
5. rejoice

3 Identification
B.

1. Polixenes
2. the shepherd
3. Florizel
4. Perdita
5. Leontes
6. Paulina
7. Antigonus
8. Camillo

4 Comprehension

1. b
2. a
3. c
4. d
5. a
6. d
7. d
8. c

P. 28 海上有這麼一座島，島上的居民只有一名叫做普洛斯的老人和他的女兒米蘭達。米蘭達是個綽約處子，稚齡之時便來到這座島上，除了父親，印象中沒再見過其他人。

　　他們住在洞窟石室裡，裡頭分成好幾個房間，其中一間做為普洛斯的書房，專為藏書之用。普洛斯大部分的書籍都跟法術有關，當時的讀書人特別著迷法術，普洛斯也發現法術很管用。他意外地漂流到這座島上時，島上被一名叫做辛蔻雷的女巫下了魔咒，在他來到島上不久前，辛蔻雷才死去。那時有一些不願為辛蔻雷幹壞事的善良精靈，被囚禁在大樹幹裡頭，普洛斯用法術把他們釋放出來，此後這些溫和的精靈就歸順了普洛斯。眾精靈的首領是艾瑞爾。

P. 29 小精靈艾瑞爾個性活潑，沒什麼壞心眼，只是愛捉弄醜怪物卡力班。他看不順眼卡力班，因為卡力班是舊仇辛蔻雷的兒子。

P. 30 卡力班一開始是在林子裡被普洛斯撿到，他長得畸形醜陋，連大猩猩都比他人模人樣。普洛斯把他帶回洞窟，教他說話，本想好好待他，怎奈母親辛蔻雷的不良遺傳，讓他什麼正事也學不會，只能做做苦工，撿撿木柴，幹幹粗活。而負責監督他工作的人正是艾瑞爾。

P. 31 如果卡力班懶惰打混，艾瑞爾（除了普洛斯，誰也看不到他）就會偷偷捏他一把，甚至把他絆倒，讓他摔進泥坑裡。接著艾瑞爾會先變成一隻大猩猩，對他扮鬼臉，再變成一隻刺蝟，在他跟前翻滾，嚇得沒穿鞋的他深怕腳會被刺到。只要他沒有力行普洛斯吩咐的工作，艾瑞爾就會用這些整人把戲來折騰他。

　　再說有了這些神通廣大的精靈們來歸順，普洛斯也能呼風喚浪了。精靈遵從他的命令捲起狂風，使得海上的一艘大船，隨時可能被巨浪吞噬。普洛斯指著船對女兒說，船上載滿的是同他們父女一樣的人類。

P. 33 女兒說道：「哦，敬愛的爸爸啊！如果是您吹起了這場可怕的風暴，就請您可憐他們的不幸吧！您看，船都快要撞得粉碎了！他們好可憐啊，會死掉的呀！要是我有能力，我要讓大海和大地乾坤移位，這樣載滿寶貴生命的船就不會被吞沒了。」

普洛斯說：「我的女兒米蘭達，妳不用怕啊，沒有人會受傷的。我已經下過命令，不可傷到船上任何一個人。我的寶貝孩子，妳可知我這麼做是為了妳啊！妳對自己或自己的身世都一無所知，對於我，你也只知道我是妳爸爸，住在這個簡陋的洞窟裡頭。妳還記得妳來到這個洞窟之前的事嗎？我想妳是不記得了，因為妳當時還不滿三歲呀。」

「爸爸，我當然記得啊！」米蘭達答道。

「記得什麼？」普洛斯問：「房子？人？孩子，跟我說妳記得什麼。」

米蘭達說：「雖然過去感覺上像是一場夢，但那時是不是有四、五個女人服侍我呢？」

普洛斯回答：「是啊，而且還不只四、五個呢。妳記憶裡的印象如何？還記得妳是怎麼來到這裡的嗎？」

「不記得了，爸爸。」米蘭達說：「我就只記得這些了。」

普洛斯說：「米蘭達啊！在十二年前，我是米蘭的公爵，妳是郡主，是我唯一的繼承人。我有個弟弟，叫做安東尼，我很信任他。因為我喜歡閉關讀書，就常把政事交給妳叔叔，也就是我那沒有道義的弟弟（他的確是沒有道義）。我醉心書堆，俗務一概不管，時間全用在修道上。我弟弟安東尼握有我的權勢，竟然就真把自己當成公爵了。我給了他親民的機會，他的壞心腸就起了壞心眼，想要奪取我的公爵的地位。不久強權敵國那不勒斯王相助舉事，他便遂其所願了。」

米蘭達問：「他們當時有想要把我們殺掉嗎？」

父親回答：「孩子，他們不敢，因為我的子民很愛戴我。安東尼要我們上一條船，行駛幾海哩後，強迫我們換搭小船，那一艘小船連根纜繩、風帆或船桅都沒有啊！他把我們丟下，以為這樣我們就活不成了。殊不知宮裡那很敬愛我的好心大臣剛則婁，偷偷在船裡擺了水、食物和衣服，還放了一些我覺得比公國都還珍貴的書呢。」

「爸爸啊！」米蘭達表示：「我那時候一定是您的拖油瓶吧？」

「才不是呢！我的寶貝。」普洛斯回答：「妳是護佑我的小天使，妳的純真笑容支撐我渡過了難關。我們漂流到這個荒島時，船上的食物都還夠用呢。米蘭達，從那時候起，我最大的快樂就是教妳學東西了，而且妳也真的學到了許多。」

「敬愛的爸爸，我對您感激不盡。」米蘭達說：「但可以請您告訴我，您現在為什麼要製造這場狂風大浪呢？」

父親回答：「好吧，我告訴妳，因為這場狂風大浪會把我的死對頭那不勒斯王和我的狠心弟弟送到島上來。」

P. 40 話一說完，精靈艾瑞爾剛好出現，準備向主人報告暴風雨的情況，說明船上的人如何被處置。因此，普洛斯就用魔杖輕點女兒，讓她沉睡過去。米蘭達看不到精靈，但普洛斯可不想讓女兒以為他在和空氣講話呢（她應該會這麼想的吧）！

普洛斯問艾瑞爾：「勇敢的精靈，你任務辦得怎麼樣了？」

艾瑞爾繪聲繪影地形容暴風雨和水手們驚恐的樣子。他說，那不勒斯王的兒子斐迪南最先躍入海裡，他父親見狀，以為兒子被海浪吞沒了。

P. 42 「但實際上他是安然無恙的。」艾瑞爾說：「他現在正在島上的某一處抱膝而坐，為父王傷心欲絕，因為他也以為父親溺死了。事實上，這位王子不但毫髮無傷，他被海浪浸濕的皇袍看起來還更光鮮了呢。」

「真是我靈敏的艾瑞爾啊！」普洛斯說：「把他帶過來，我女兒要見見這位年輕王子。國王和我弟弟又在哪裡呢？」

艾瑞爾回答：「我讓他們忙著尋找斐迪南。他們親眼看到他落水，只能絕望地尋找他。船上沒有半個人失蹤，但每個人都以為自己是唯一的生還者。他們的船也安安穩穩地停靠在岸邊，只是他們看不到。」

「艾瑞爾啊！」普洛斯說：「你的任務已經圓滿達成，不過還有其他差事。」

「還有其他差事？」艾瑞爾說：「主人，容我提醒您，您答應過要還我自由的。請您想想，我為您效勞，任勞任怨，從不說謊犯錯呀！」

P. 44 「現在是怎麼了？」普洛斯說：「你忘了你是在什麼樣水深火熱的痛苦中被我救出來的嗎？你忘了年老善妒、彎腰駝背的邪惡女巫辛蔻雷了嗎？回答我，辛蔻雷是在哪裡出生的？」

「大人，她在阿爾及爾出生。」艾瑞爾回答。

17

「哦，是嗎？」普洛斯說：「看來你是忘了，我得把你的來歷再說一遍。邪惡的辛蔻雷女巫因為使用駭人聽聞的法術，被驅逐出阿爾及爾，水手們就把她流放到這個島上來。你是個善巧精靈，不肯服從惡毒的命令，所以就被她鎖在樹幹裡頭。我發現你的時候，你正苦苦哀號著呢！你可得記好，是我把你從這種苦難中救出來的。」

「敬愛的主人，您原諒我呀！」艾瑞爾為自己的忘恩負義感到羞愧，他說：「我會對您唯命是從的。」

普洛斯說：「你服從我，我就會還你自由。」說完就指示下一步命令。艾瑞爾離開後，前往剛剛丟下斐迪南的地方，而斐迪南仍憂心悄悄地坐在草地上。

P. 46 「年輕的紳士啊！」艾瑞爾對著他說：「我現在要帶你走，好讓米蘭達小姐瞧瞧你的俏臉蛋。你得跟我走，走吧，先生，跟我走吧。」說完他接著唱：

令尊葬身五噚海底；
他骨骼化成珊瑚石；
他眼睛變成珍珠粒：
全身完好無一腐爛，
變幻瑰麗又甚奇妙。
海仙子時時敲喪鐘：
聽！我聞它叮噹響。

P. 48 父親的這個噩耗甚是古怪，王子從失神的狀態中驚醒過來。他心下詫異，跟著艾瑞爾的聲音走，直到碰見坐在大樹蔭影下的普洛斯和米蘭達。現在，米蘭達終於見到父親以外的第一個人類。

普洛斯問：「米蘭達，妳盯著那邊看是在看什麼呀？」

「爸爸！」米蘭達露出前所未有的訝異神情，說道：「想必他是個精靈吧！啊，你看他東張西望的樣子！爸爸，真的，他真的是個美麗的動物。他是精靈吧？」

「女兒，他不是精靈。」父親回答：「他會吃會睡，跟我們一樣有知覺。他本來是那條船上的人，現在因為傷心而變得憔悴，

18

要不然可稱得上是潘安再世喔！他和船上的其他人失散，正到處尋找他們。」

P. 50 米蘭達還以為所有男人都長得跟她父親一樣，一臉嚴肅表情，蓄著灰鬍鬚。現在看到這位俊美的年輕王子，不禁心神舒暢。再說斐迪南，在這荒地看到如此花容月貌的女子，又聽到剛剛那些奇幻聲音，彷彿身置奇境仙鄉，以為自己到了仙島，逕自把米蘭達當成女神，稱她是女神地講起話來了。

　　米蘭達羞怯地表示自己不是女神，只是個普通的姑娘。她正要自我介紹時，普洛斯插斷她的話。普洛斯樂見他們相互傾心，一眼就瞧出他們彼此一見鍾情（就像我們說的）。但為了考驗斐迪南的忠貞，他決定故意為難他們。他走向他們，嚴詞厲色地誣賴王子來島上是為了當間諜，想從他這個島主的手中把島奪走。

P. 52 「你跟我來！」普洛斯說：「我要把你的脖子和兩腳綁在一塊，你只能喝海水，吃貝類動物、枯樹根和橡果殼。」

　　斐迪南回答：「休想，除非你打贏我，要不然我是不會乖乖就範的。」說完便拔出劍，誰知普洛斯魔杖一揮，他的雙腳就黏在地上，動也動不了了。

　　米蘭達抓住父親的手，說道：「爸爸，為何要這麼殘暴啊！可憐可憐他吧！我可以擔保，這是我今生第二個見到的男人，看來是個正人君子啊。」

P. 53 父親回答：「女兒，你住口，你再多嘴我就罵妳！怎麼啦，想袒護騙徒嗎？妳只見過他和卡力班這兩個人，就以為他們的為人再好不過了嗎？傻丫頭，他比卡力班好很多是吧？我告訴妳，大部分的男人又要比他好很多。」

　　普洛斯這麼說，也是為考驗女兒的忠誠。未料女兒回答：「我對感情要求不多，就算有人比他更好，我也沒興趣。」

　　「來吧，小伙子！」普洛斯對王子說：「你沒能耐抵抗我的。」

P. 54 「我的確是沒有。」斐迪南回答。他不知道自己被施了法，完全失去了反抗力量。他很詫異，自己竟莫名其妙、不由自主地跟著普洛斯走。他回頭望著米蘭達，直到看不見了為止。他跟著普洛斯走進洞窟，說道：「我好像在做夢，我的心被控制住了。不過，只要我在囚室裡能每天望著那名美麗女子一回，那麼，眼前這個人的威脅，或是我自己的無能為力，我都不當一回事了。」

19

普洛斯囚禁斐迪南沒多久，就把他帶出來，派給他困難的差事。普洛斯故意也讓女兒知道是什麼樣的差事後，就假裝走進書房，實則暗中觀察兩人。

P. 56 普洛斯給斐迪南的差事是要他把一些笨重的木頭堆起來。這個國王的公子可不習慣這種粗活呀，米蘭達很快發現這個她鍾愛的人會累得出人命。

「哎呀！」她說：「你犯不著這麼賣力的啊！我爸在看書，三個小時內都不會出來的，請你休息一下吧！」

「敬愛的小姐呀！」斐迪南說：「我不敢，我要完成工作之後才休息。」

米蘭達說：「你坐下休息，換我來搬木頭吧！」

斐迪南不肯答應。這下米蘭達反而幫了倒忙，因為他們沒完沒了地聊起天來，結果木頭搬得還真得有夠慢。

普洛斯要斐迪南做粗活，是想試煉他的愛情。他並不如女兒所說的是在看書，而是躲在一旁偷聽他們講話。

斐迪南問她芳名，她告訴了他，還說父親不准她跟人報上自己的名字。

P. 58 看到女兒這初次的違逆，普洛斯笑了笑，畢竟正是他用法術讓女兒乍時墜入情網的，所以不會生氣女兒為了愛情而違背他的命令。他也很得意地聽著斐迪南的一番傾訴，因為男方告訴女兒，說她是他這輩子最愛的女人。

P. 59 米蘭達聽到斐迪南歌頌她的美貌，說她絕色無雙，便說道：「我腦海裡沒有任何女人的影像，而且除了你這位好友和我敬愛的父親，我也沒見過其他男人。我不知道島外的人長得如何，但你要相信我，先生，在這世上我只想和你作伴。除了你，我再也想像不出還有什麼樣的容貌會讓我動心。先生啊，我說得太露骨了，把父親的訓誡都給忘了。」

聽到這裡，普洛斯頷首笑了笑，彷彿是說：「事情進行得正合我意啊，我女兒就要成為那不勒斯的皇后了。」

P. 60 斐迪南又一番傾訴心曲，年輕王子講話果然就像個王子，他跟純真的米蘭達說，他是那不勒斯的王位繼承人，所以她會成為他的皇后。

「啊，先生！」她説：「我真傻，竟然為高興的事情掉眼淚。我坦白、天真無邪地回答你，如果你要娶我，我就是你的妻子了。」

也不等斐迪南對米蘭達表示感激，普洛斯驀地出現。

「別怕，孩子。」他説：「你們剛才所説的話我都聽到了，我很贊成。斐迪南，如果我苛待你，那就讓我把女兒許配給你來做為補償。我找些事情來刁難你，只是想考驗你的愛情，現在你已經光榮通過考驗了。接受我的女兒吧，就當作是我送給你的禮物，這是你真心真意的愛情所應該得的報償。你不要笑我是老王賣瓜，事實上無論你怎麼讚美她，都還沒有實際的她好呢！」

P. 61 接著，普洛斯説他得親自去處理一些事情，盼他們坐下來聊聊天，等他回來。看來，米蘭達一點也不想違抗這個命令了。

普洛斯離開後就把精靈艾瑞爾給召來，艾瑞爾旋即出現，趕著説明自己如何處理普洛斯的弟弟和那不勒斯王。

艾瑞爾説他用異象幻聽，嚇得他們幾乎魂不附體。他們四處走，累了餓了時，他就忽地在他們面前變幻出餐宴美食。待他們著手要吃時，他就變化成長著翅膀、貪得無厭的鳥身女妖出現，美食也頓時消失。

P. 63 而最令他們驚恐的是，鳥身女妖跟他們説，他們狠心把普洛斯趕出公國，讓普洛斯和襁褓中的幼女葬身海底，而他們之所以會遇到今天這些恐怖的事情，就是因為幹了那些勾當。

那不勒斯王和不義兄弟安東尼聽了懊悔不已，後悔對普洛斯不仁不義。艾瑞爾告訴主人，他確信他們真心悔過，連他這個精靈也忍不住同情他們。

「艾瑞爾，那就把他們帶來吧。」普洛斯説：「你一個精靈都能感受到他們的痛楚了，和他們一樣同是人類的我，能不發點慈悲嗎？快把他們帶過來吧，可愛的艾瑞爾。」

艾瑞爾隨即在天上奏起奇妙樂聲，把國王、安東尼、老剛則妻等一行人，誘引到主人面前。這名剛則妻就是當年好心為普洛斯準備書物的那名剛則妻，那時狠心的弟弟把普洛斯扔在無一遮蔽物的小船上，要讓他在海上命喪九泉。

P. 64 悲痛恐懼懾住眾人，他們沒認出來普洛斯。普洛斯走到好心的老剛則妻面前，稱他是救命恩人，這時弟弟和國王才認出原來他就是當年受害的普洛斯。

21

安東尼涕泗交流，誠心痛悔，請求哥哥原諒，國王也實著後悔幫助了安東尼竊奪兄長的爵位。普洛斯原諒了他們。在他們保證歸還爵位時，普洛斯告訴那不勒斯王說：「我也有禮相贈。」普洛斯話一說完就打了開門，讓國王看看正在和米蘭達下棋的兒子斐迪南。

P. 65 再沒有比父子意外重逢更激動人心的事了，他們一度以為對方都在風暴雨中溺斃了。

　　「太奇妙了！」米蘭達說：「這些人類多高貴啊！他們住在那裡，那裡必然是個美麗世界呀！」

P. 67 看到眼前這位絕色佳麗米蘭達，那不勒斯王和兒子一樣目瞪口呆。他問：「這位姑娘是誰啊？是讓我們離散又重聚的女神嗎？」

　　斐迪南回答：「爸爸，不是的。」看到父親跟自己一樣，初見她時就把她當作是女神，不禁莞爾一笑。他解釋：「她是個凡人，但上帝把她賜給了我。爸爸，我未經您同意就決定娶她，是因為我沒有想到您還活著啊。她是有名的米蘭公爵普洛斯的女兒，我早已久仰其大名，現在終於見到他的盧山真面目了。他讓我重獲新生，可說是我的第二個父親，因為他把這位可愛的姑娘許配給了我。」

　　「那我就是她的父親了囉！」國王說：「不過這聽來好奇怪啊，我得請求我這個孩子原諒我。」

　　「休提這些了！」普洛斯說：「如今一切圓滿，就把舊日嫌隙都忘了吧！」

P. 68 普洛斯抱住弟弟，重申自己已經原諒她了，還說充滿智慧、主宰萬物的神，之所以讓他被驅逐出可憐的米蘭公國，乃是為了爾後讓女兒得以繼承那不勒斯王位。正因這座荒島，他們兩人才相遇，王子才愛上米蘭達的。

　　普洛斯特意講好話來安慰弟弟，羞悔不已的安東尼泣不成聲。看到這種圓滿和解，好心的老剛則婁也感動得落淚，祈求蒼天保佑這對年輕情侶。

　　普洛斯告訴他們，他們的船很安全地停在岸邊，水手都在船上，明早，他就會和女兒同他們一道回家。

　　他說：「這會兒，就到我的洞窟寒舍休息休息，吃點東西吧。我來說說我到了這荒島之後的生活，好當作今晚的餘興節目。」

22

P. 69 他吩咐卡力班準備食物，收拾洞窟。看到這個醜八怪笨拙的動作和粗野的外形，眾人無不咋舌。普洛斯則表示，這是他唯一的僕人了。

離開荒島之前，普洛斯還給了艾瑞爾自由身，讓這個活潑的小精靈好不雀躍。雖然他一向對主人忠心耿耿，但總是渴望享受無拘無束的自由，可以像隻野鳥在綠林香果間、芬芳花叢上自由翱翔。

P. 71 在還給他自由時，普洛斯說：「古靈精怪的艾瑞爾啊！儘管我會懷念你，但你仍應去享受自由。」

「謝謝您，敬愛的主人！」艾瑞爾說：「但請先讓我用順風護送您的船回家，然後您再向幫助過您的這個忠實精靈道別吧！主人，等我自由了，我會過得很快樂的！」艾瑞爾接著歡唱了這首悅耳的歌曲：

P. 72
> 蜜蜂吮蜜處我同吮吮；
> 野櫻草花瓣間我棲身；
> 貓頭鷹啼叫時我蹲伏。
> 乘著蝙蝠背脊我飛舞，
> 但且心神俱暢逐夏日。
> 從今以後我要樂陶陶，
> 枝頭花朵堆下過生活。

P. 73 最後，普洛斯把魔法書和魔杖深埋地底下，決心收山不再碰法術。他制勝敵人，和弟弟與那不勒斯王言歸於好，已經了無遺憾。現在只待返鄉，重收公國，參加女兒和王子斐迪南喜氣洋洋的婚禮。國王說，待他們一回那不勒斯，即舉行隆重婚禮。

在精靈艾瑞爾的平安護送下，他們一路旅程愉快，不久重回那不勒斯。

《冬天的故事》中譯

P. 90　西西里國王雷提斯和德貌雙全的王后荷麥妮，有過一段琴瑟和鳴的日子。擁有這麼出色的夫人，雷提斯萬般幸福，一切稱心如意，只是有時懸念再見波希米亞國王波利茲這位老同窗，也好讓他認識認識自己的皇后。

P. 91　雷提斯和波利茲兩人穿著同一條開襠褲長大，可惜在他們父王死後，就各自被召回去統治王國。雖然雙方常交流貢品、信函和大使，但兩人已經好幾年沒見過面了。

最後，一再邀請之下，波利茲終於從波希米亞來到西西里宮廷拜訪好友雷提斯。

一開始，這件事讓雷提斯雀躍不已。他請王后要特別招待他這位兒時同伴，能和死黨老友相聚首，他感到非常興奮。他們聊起舊日時光，回憶學生時代和年輕時玩過的把戲，並說給始終興致昂昂在旁聆聽的皇后荷麥妮聽。

P. 92　住了好一陣子之後，波利茲準備啟程告辭，雷提斯要荷麥妮和他一塊請波利茲再多留幾天。

未料這件事竟成為好皇后傷心的肇端，因為波利茲原本拒絕雷提斯，卻被她的溫柔勸說給打動，決定留下來多待幾個星期。

儘管雷提斯熟知好友波利茲為人正直，行事光明磊落，也明白賢德王后的品行絕佳，卻仍起了無可遏止的嫉妒心。

P. 94　荷麥妮按丈夫的要求善待波利茲，為只為討丈夫歡心，未料卻反而讓這可悲的國王更加妒火中燒。國王原本是位熱情忠貞的朋友，也是個最好、最溫柔的丈夫，卻在轉眼間變成一頭凶猛蠻橫的怪物。他差來宮裡的勛爵卡密羅，跟他說心裡頭的疑忌，要他去把波利茲毒死。

卡密羅心眼好，他很清楚雷提斯根本只是在亂吃飛醋，所以不但沒有下毒加害波利茲，還把國王主子的命令告訴了他，然後同意和他一起逃出西西里國境。在卡密羅的幫助下，波利茲安全回到自己的波希米亞王國。此後卡密羅就留在這位國王的宮廷裡，成為波利茲的至交和愛臣。

P. 96　波利茲一逃走，嫉妒的雷提斯更加大為光火。他跑去皇后的

24

寝宮，逢見善良的夫人和小兒子馬密利並肩而坐，馬密利正準備講他最得意的故事，來讓母親開心。未料國王一進來，就把孩子帶走，兀自將荷麥妮打入大牢。

P. 98　年幼的馬密利摯愛著母親，他看到她受到這樣侮辱，被人從他身旁給拉進牢裡，好不傷心。他漸漸消沉，日形憔悴，食不下嚥，睡不成眠，恐會悲傷而死。

P. 99　把皇后關進牢裡後，雷提斯派了克里歐和迪翁這兩名西西里勛爵，到德爾菲的阿波羅神廟求神諭，想知道皇后是否對他不忠。

　　進了牢裡沒多久，荷麥妮生下一女。看著可愛的嬰兒，可憐的夫人感到安慰多了。她對孩子說：「我可憐的小囚犯，我和你一樣無辜啊！」

　　荷麥妮有個性格高尚的好友寶琳娜，寶琳娜是西西里勛爵安提貢的妻子，她一聽說皇后生子，就前去荷麥妮受禁的地牢，對服侍荷麥妮的愛蜜莉說：「愛蜜莉，請你去跟皇后說，如果她信得過我，我就帶嬰兒到她父王那邊，說不定他看了這無辜的孩子就會心軟了。」

P. 100　愛蜜莉回答：「可敬的夫人呀，我會跟皇后說這個好主意的，她今天還希望有朋友敢把小孩帶給國王呢！」

　　寶琳娜說：「妳跟她說，我會為她跟雷提斯辯解求情的。」

　　「妳對慈愛的皇后這麼好，願上帝永遠保佑妳啊！」

　　愛蜜莉說完即去找荷麥妮。荷麥妮興奮地把嬰兒交給寶琳娜，她還擔心沒有人敢把小孩帶給國王呢！

　　寶琳娜抱著這個初生的小嬰兒要去見國王，她丈夫害怕她會激怒國王，便一路阻擋她。然而她硬是闖到國王面前，把小孩放在國王腳邊，然後義正嚴詞地為荷麥妮辯護。她痛斥國王沒人性，懇求他放過這對無辜的母女。

P. 102　寶琳娜激昂的諫言惹得雷提斯更加不悅，便命令她丈夫安提貢把她帶下去。

　　寶琳娜把小嬰兒留在嬰兒父親的腳邊，逕自離開。她想，等他們一獨處，他看過孩子之後，就會為她的清白無辜動容了。

　　只可惜好心的寶琳娜估錯算盤。她人才一離開，這位狠心的父親就要她丈夫安提貢把孩子帶出海，扔到無人的岸上，讓她自生自滅。

安提貢不比好心腸的卡密羅。他對雷提斯言聽計從，立刻就搭船帶孩子出海，準備一遇見荒岸，就把她扔下。

P. 104 國王一味認定荷麥妮對他不忠，也不等去德爾菲的阿波羅廟求神諭的克里歐和迪翁回來，在皇后產後身子尚虛，還在為失去寶貝女兒而傷心之際，就把她押到朝廷上，當著朝臣貴族的面前公開審判她。

P. 105 國內眾大臣法官等貴族都到齊來勘審荷麥妮，這位憂悒的皇后囚犯站在眾人面前，等待判決。就在這時，克里歐和迪翁走進議會，把密封的神諭結果上呈國王。雷提斯命人拆封，將神諭大聲讀出來。神諭上寫著：

荷麥妮清清白白，

波利茲無可指責，

卡密羅一介忠臣，

雷提斯善妒暴君。

若不尋回被棄者，

國王身後無可繼。

P. 106 怎奈國王就是不相信這則神諭。他說這是皇后的親信所編造出來的，要法官繼續審問皇后。雷提斯話猶未了，但見一人走進來稟告說，馬密利王子因為聽到母親要被判死罪，竟悲羞得暴斃了。

P. 107 一聽到這個情深的愛子為自己的不幸傷心而亡，荷麥妮暈厥了過去。這個消息也讓雷提斯萬分錐心，開始對不幸的皇后起了憐憫心。他命令寶琳娜和皇后的宮娥們把皇后帶下去，想辦法讓她清醒。

一會兒後，寶琳娜回來稟報國王，說荷麥妮已經香消玉殞。

聽到皇后的噩耗，雷提斯這才悔恨自己對她太狠心，心想自己對她的虐待一定傷透了她的心。他現在相信了她的清白，也相信神諭所言真實。他想，神諭上所言的「若不尋回被棄者」，指的應該就是他的小女兒，畢竟小王子馬密利已經不在人間，他沒有其他子嗣了。現在，他倒願意用他的王國來換回被棄的女兒。他自責不已，在悲傷悔恨中度過了許多年。

安提貢帶著尚在襁褓中的公主出海的船，因為一場暴風雨被吹到波希米亞境內的海岸上，那裡正是正直國王波利茲的王國。上岸後，安提貢扔下小嬰兒逕自離去。

P.109 結果，安提貢再也沒有回到西西里向雷提斯申奏公主被棄的地點，因為當他要返回船上時，林子裡跑出一隻熊，把他撕個稀爛。他依雷提斯那個沒天良的命令行事，這是他應得的懲罰呀。

荷麥妮要讓小女兒去見雷提斯時，精心為她穿戴了華服寶飾。安提貢則在她的斗篷別上一張紙，寫著「帕蒂坦」這個名字，還有幾句暗示她出身高貴和遭遇不幸的話。

P.111 這名可憐的棄嬰後來被一個牧羊人發現。牧羊人心腸好，把小帕蒂坦帶回家讓老婆悉心養育。他人窮，不想讓別人知道他撿到珠寶，就搬離原本居住的地方，以免被人知道他是在哪兒發了財。他拿了帕蒂坦的一些珠寶去買了羊，成為一名有錢的牧羊人。

他把帕蒂坦視如己出地撫養長大，帕蒂坦也一直認為自己就是牧羊人的女兒。

P.112 小帕蒂坦出落得亭亭玉立。她所受的教養是一般牧羊人家給女兒的教養，但璞玉未琢的她，畢竟有母后高貴天性的遺傳。她的舉止儀態，會讓人以為她根本就是在親生父親的皇宮裡長大的。

波希米亞國王波利茲有個獨子，叫做弗羅瑞。一次，這位年輕王子在牧羊人家附近打獵時，瞥見了老牧羊人這位所謂的女兒。帕蒂坦的美麗、靦腆和尊貴的氣質，霎時讓他一見鐘情。

P.113 不久王子假扮成平民，取名多里克，常跑去老牧羊人家逗留。波利茲發現弗羅瑞常常不在宮中，便要人監督他兒子，結果得知弗羅瑞原來是迷戀上牧羊人的美麗女兒。

波利茲召來曾把他從雷提斯手中救出來的忠臣卡密羅，要卡密羅陪他去找帕蒂坦的牧羊人父親。

P.115 喬裝過的波利茲和卡密羅來到老牧羊人的家裡時，人們正在舉行剪羊毛儀式。因逢盛會，他們這兩個陌生人受到歡迎，被邀請進屋，參加慶典活動。

整個活動好不歡樂。人們擺好桌子，備好上等酒菜，慶祝農家盛宴。有些少男少女在屋前的綠地上歡舞，有些年輕人在門口跟小販買絲帶、手套等這類的小玩意兒。

P.117 在這熱鬧的氣氛中，弗羅瑞和帕蒂坦卻獨坐在一旁的角落裡。與其加入周圍鬧哄哄的娛樂活動，他們似乎更喜歡和彼此聊天談心。

國王經過喬裝，兒子認不出他，他便趁機走近兩人，偷聽他們談話。看到和兒子說話的帕蒂坦單純又優雅，波利茲很是訝異。他對卡密羅說：「我從沒見過這麼漂亮而出身低下的姑娘，她說話和表現出來的樣子都不像是這種出身的人，她的高貴和這個地方一點也不相稱呀。」

P. 118 卡密羅答道：「的確，她可說是牧羊人之后啊！」

「請問你，好心的朋友。」國王問老牧羊人說：「正在跟你女兒講話的俊俏年輕人是誰呀？」

牧羊人回答：「他叫多里克。他說他愛上我女兒，但老實說，你看他們兩人親嘴的樣子，誰也不會愛得比誰少啊！多里克這孩子要是真能娶到她，她會帶給他意想不到的福氣呢！」老牧人指的是帕蒂坦剩下的珠寶。他拿一些珠寶來買羊群，剩下的珠寶他就小心保管，以便給她當嫁妝。

P. 119 波利茲接著對兒子說：「小伙子，現在是怎麼回事？」他說：「你的魂好像被攝走了，無心參加宴會。我年輕的時候，常常送禮物給情人，而你竟然那樣就讓小販走了，也不給你的情人買些什麼。」

年輕的王子完全沒料到跟他說話的是父王。他答道：「老先生啊，帕蒂坦不在乎這些小玩意，她想要的禮物是鎖在我心頭裡的東西。」

他說罷，便轉向帕蒂坦，說道：「帕蒂坦，這位老生先想必也曾是個多情人。現在當著他的面，請妳聽我的告白吧，也讓他聽聽我是怎麼說的。」

P. 120 弗羅瑞要向帕蒂坦鄭重求婚，他請這個陌生老翁作證人。他對波利茲說：「請您為我們證婚吧！」

「我看是為你們的分手作證吧，小伙子！」國王現出真正的身分。

P. 121 波利茲斥責兒子竟敢和出身卑微的女孩訂婚，又用「牧羊崽子」、「羊鉤子」等輕蔑的稱呼來叫帕蒂坦，還威脅她要是再跟他兒子見面，就要把她和她的老牧羊人父親處死。

國王說完後，氣沖沖地離開，命令卡密羅帶王子弗羅瑞隨後跟上。

　　國王的責罵倒是凸顯了帕蒂坦高貴的本性，他離開後，帕蒂坦說：「雖然我們的關係完了，但我不怕。剛剛我有一兩次都很想插話，很想明白地告訴他，照耀他皇宮的太陽，同樣也照耀我們的小茅屋，它可是一視同仁的。」

P. 123 她接著悲傷地說：「但現在我是大夢初醒了，我再也不會自詡為女王了。先生，你走吧，我要去擠羊奶，然後邊掉淚。」

　　好心腸的卡密羅深為帕蒂坦的特質和得體的舉止所吸引，而且他也看出來，深愛她的年輕王子是不會為了父命而放棄她。這時他心生良策，不但可以幫助這對情侶，還可以實現他心裡盼想的計畫呢。

　　卡密羅早就知道西西里國王雷提斯已經真心悔過，儘管他現在是波利茲國王的至交，他仍渴望再見到以前服侍過的國王和故鄉。他建議弗羅瑞和帕蒂坦跟他一起回西西里宮廷，並擔保雷提斯會保護他們，由雷提斯出面調解，直到波利茲寬恕他們並答應婚事。

P. 124 他們很高興地接受了這個建議。卡密羅安排潛逃的一切事宜，並答應讓老牧羊人和他們一起上路。

　　老牧羊人隨身帶上帕蒂坦剩下的珠寶，還有嬰兒裝和別在斗篷上的紙條。

　　他們沿途平順，弗羅瑞、帕蒂坦、卡密羅和老牧羊人一行人，最後平安地來到雷提斯的宮殿。此時雷提斯仍為死去的荷麥妮和棄子哀傷。他殷勤接待卡密羅，也熱誠歡迎弗羅瑞王子。

　　然而當弗羅瑞以王妃的身分介紹帕蒂坦時，他看得目瞪口呆──帕蒂坦和死去的荷麥妮長得如此相似，讓他不禁悲從中來。他說，如果當初沒有狠心殺掉女兒，那女兒現在也是這樣一位可愛的姑娘了。

P. 126 他對弗羅瑞說：「而且，我還和你賢明的父親斷絕來往，失去彼此的友誼。現在，只要能再見到他，我死也甘願啊！」

　　國王這麼注意帕蒂坦，又說曾失去一個在襁褓裡就被丟棄的女兒，老牧羊人於是算算他撿到小帕蒂坦的時間，再想想她遭棄時的樣子，還有其他象徵貴族出身的珠寶等等，最後他不得不推論出：帕蒂坦就是國王的女兒。

老牧羊人向國王稟奏他撿到孩子的經過，弗羅瑞、帕蒂坦、卡密羅和忠誠的寶琳娜都在旁聆聽。他還描述了安提貢遇難時的情況，說他目睹了熊撲在安提貢的身上。

P. 127 之後他拿出一件華麗的斗篷，寶琳娜認出來那就是荷麥妮用來包裹孩子的斗篷。他又拿出一件珠寶，她也記得荷麥妮曾將它掛在帕蒂坦的頸子上。最後他拿出紙條，寶琳娜認出那是丈夫的筆跡。這一下子，帕蒂坦無疑就是雷提斯的親生女兒！但是，唉！寶琳娜內心裡衝突不已呀，她既為丈夫的死而悲傷，又為神諭的應驗而高興：這下國王終於找到繼承人，找回他當初遺棄的女兒了。

聽到帕蒂坦就是自己的女兒，又想到過世的荷麥妮看不到親生孩子，雷提斯悲慟得久久不能言語，只說出：「啊！妳的母親，妳的母親！」

P. 128 在這悲喜交集之際，寶琳娜插話對雷提斯說，她有座雕像，最近才剛由優異的義大利大師朱利諾‧羅馬諾所完成。那座雕像和皇后維妙維肖，要是國王陛下肯去她家瞧瞧，一定也會以為那就是荷麥妮本人。於是眾人便出發前往她家，國王迫不及待想看長得和荷麥妮一模一樣的雕像，帕蒂坦也渴望知道未曾謀面的母親的樣子。

P. 130 寶琳娜把遮蓋美麗雕像的帷幕拉開。看到雕像和荷麥妮如此神似，國王的悲傷全湧了上來，好一段時間都說不出話，只是木然不動。

「國王陛下，看您一語不發，我倒高興，這表示您真的很驚訝呢。您看，這雕像是不是很像皇后啊！」寶琳娜說。

國王終於開口道：「啊！我當初向她求婚時，她就是站這個樣子的，是這樣的雍容華貴啊！可是寶琳娜妳看，雕像看起來比荷麥妮老呀！」

寶琳娜答道：「這正是雕刻師傅厲害的地方啊，他把雕像雕得栩栩如生。陛下，我要把帷幕放下了，免得您等一下還以為它會動呢！」

國王說：「不要把帷幕放下，除非我死了！卡密羅你看，你不覺得她好像會呼吸嗎？她的眼睛好像在動呢！」

P. 131 「國王陛下，我真的要把帷幕放下了啦！」寶琳娜說：「您

30

看得太出神了，會誤以為雕像是活的。」

「啊，親愛的寶琳娜。」雷提斯說：「那就讓我接下來的二十年都這麼想吧！我仍能感覺到她的氣息。有什麼鬼斧神工可以連呼吸都刻得出來呢？誰都不准笑我，我要去親吻她。」

P.133 「啊！陛下！那不成啊！」寶琳娜說：「雕像嘴唇上的紅漆還沒乾呢，您的唇會沾上油彩的。我可以把帷幕放下了嗎？」

「不行，二十年之內都不准放下。」雷提斯說。

始終跪在一旁的帕蒂坦，靜靜仰望著完美無瑕的母親雕像。她說：「我也可以在這裡待上二十年，一直望著我親愛的母親。」

「你們兩個都不要再胡思亂想了。」寶琳娜對雷提斯說：「讓我把帷幕放下吧，免得您還會更吃驚！我可以讓雕像移動，叫它從座台上走下來，牽您的手。不過您一定會以為是什麼妖術在幫我，我先聲明我可沒有。」

國王驚訝地說：「不管妳叫它做什麼，我都很想看。如果妳讓她說話，我也很想聽。妳要是能讓她動，也就能讓她講話吧。」

P.135 寶琳娜命人奏起預先就準備好的莊嚴慢樂。只但見眾人驚訝不已，因為雕像竟從座台上走了下來。它用手臂摟住雷提斯的脖子，並說話來為丈夫和剛剛找回的孩子帕蒂坦祈願祝福。

難怪雕像會摟著雷提斯的脖子，會保佑丈夫和孩子。也難怪呀，因為這座雕像就是荷麥妮本人，是如假包換、活生生的皇后。

寶琳娜向國王謊報荷麥妮的死訊，是因為心想只有這個辦法可以保住皇后的性命。此後，荷麥妮就住在好心的寶琳娜那裡。要不是聽說已經找到帕蒂坦，荷麥妮也不會讓雷提斯知道她還活著。雖然她早就原諒雷提斯帶給她的傷害，卻無法原諒他那樣狠心對待襁褓中的女兒。

P.136 死去的皇后復活，被棄的女兒尋回，悲傷已久的雷提斯欣喜欲狂。

各方無不捎來祝賀和熱切的問候。這對父母開心地感謝弗羅瑞王子對女兒的愛，她一度只是出身卑微的女孩。他們也祝福好心的老牧羊人，他搭救扶養了他們的孩子。卡密羅和寶琳娜也好不歡喜，可以親眼看到自己的盡忠效力得到了這樣的好結局。

這時，像是為了使這奇異意外的喜悅更加圓滿似的，波利茲國王也來到了皇宮。

卡密羅早渴望歸鄉，當初兒子和卡密羅失蹤時，波利茲就料想可以在西西里找到這兩個人。他全速追趕他們，剛好在雷提斯一生最快樂的時刻裡趕到。

P.137 波利茲與大家同樂，他原諒好友雷提斯對他亂吃飛醋，兩人再度重修舊好，就像小時候那樣相親相愛。現在再也不用擔心波利茲會反對兒子娶帕蒂坦了，帕蒂坦也不再是什麼羊鉤子，而是西西里的皇位繼承人了。

　　我們看到具有堅忍德性的荷麥妮，長年受苦之後終於得到報償。這個完美的女性和雷提斯及帕蒂坦一起過了好多年，這一下她可是最幸福的母親和皇后了。